Puffin Books
Editor: *Kaye Webb*
P S 342
Hell's Edge

'Hell's Edge' is the nickname of a smoky Yorkshire town where Ril Terry comes to live with her father. She hates everything compared with her old home and school. Even her cousin Norman, who might have been fun, is sulky and awkward, and scoffs at her taste for history. What Norman wants is to be a car mechanic.

Ril soon finds out about the old feud between their ancestor Caradoc Clough and the local landowners the Withens, who had enclosed Hallersage's common land long ago, so that now there is no open ground for the people of Hallersage to amuse themselves. At last she and Norman are united by their struggle to get back the land, but not without far-reaching and painful results.

Hell's Edge has been widely praised as a perceptive book about modern, independent young people, and was a runner-up for the Carnegie Medal in 1963.
'Full of vivid people and vigorous dialogue' – Edward Blishen in the *Guardian*

Cover design by Douglas Hall

HELL'S EDGE

JOHN ROWE TOWNSEND

PENGUIN BOOKS

by arrangement with
Hutchinson of London

Penguin Books Ltd, Harmondsworth,
Middlesex, England
Penguin Books Inc., 3300 Clipper Mill Road,
Baltimore, Md 21211, U.S.A.
Penguin Books Australia Ltd, Ringwood,
Victoria, Australia

First published by Hutchinson 1963
Published in Puffin Books 1968
Copyright © John Rowe Townsend, 1963

Made and printed in Great Britain by
C. Nicholls & Company Ltd,
Set in Linotype Juliana

1

'When I was your age,' said Florrie Clough grimly, 'I 'ad to do what I was told, an' no arguin', or me dad'd 'ave bin after me wi' t'strap.'

'When you was my age,' said her son Norman, 'things was different.'

'They was an' all. Six of us int' family, an' we didn't make half o' t'muck an' noise an' argument that your dad an' me get from one lad of fifteen.'

'Oh aye, them were t'days,' said Norman. 'When young-sters knew their place – or so you keep tellin' me.'

'There you are ! More cheek ! You'll be callin' your mum a liar next.'

'No, I don't mean that. But I wonder if things was quite like you remember them, that's all.'

'Well, I can tell you this,' said Florrie, 'an' just pass me them plates, will you, it's time I was gettin' on wi' t'washin'-up. I can tell you this, Norman Clough, if my mum 'ad asked me to go an' meet a new cousin that was comin' up from t'South, I'd 'ave done it like a shot without all this fuss.'

'I've told you, Mum,' said Norman patiently, 'I promised to go round t'garage to work on that car Roy bought yester-day. 'E's sold it already, and t'customer wants to collect it tomorrow mornin', an' it isn't fit to be on t'road.'

'Garage ! Garage ! You might as well go an' live at that garage !'

Florrie swept up a tray of tea-things and marched into the scullery of the little house in Hallersage. She was a thick-set, capable, house-proud woman with a high

The Withens
Wall

Withishall

River Haller

Station

Hallersage
Grammar School

Park
Terrace

Milton
St

HALLERSAGE
TOWN CENTRE

Old Hallersage Rd

Leeds Rd

Derby Road

Old Hallersage
Market Place

Pennine Road

N

Built-up
area

Moors

Main
roads

Railway

Map of the West Riding Town of
HALLERSAGE
commonly known as
'Hell's Edge'

complexion and a sharp tongue – 'but she's good-'earted, like', the neighbours would say when they talked about her.

'I can't think why you don't do as she says,' grumbled Fred Clough. 'Keep 'er quiet. She'll be on at us all day if you don't.'

Fred was a tall, thin, mournful-looking man with a little moustache. His son ignored his remark.

Florrie's voice floated in from the scullery.

'And another thing,' she went on. 'If you spent less time at that garage you might get on better with your lessons.'

'Aw, come off it, Mum !' said Norman. He got up from his chair and stood in the scullery doorway.

Florrie looked at him with annoyance mingled with pride. He was a tall, thin-faced, good-looking boy with dark wavy hair. Soon he'd be needing a shave. A fine lad, thought Florrie, for all his awkwardness; and good to his mother, too, which was more than you could say for a lot of Hallersage lads these days.

'Give us that pot-cloth,' he said. 'I'll dry for you. Then I'm goin' out.'

He met Florrie's look halfway.

'An' don't start on to me about 'omework. There isn't any tonight, seein' it's exam time.'

''Ow often do you do it, anyway?' demanded Florrie.

'Too often. I've 'ad enough of it. I've 'ad enough of school, if you want to know. I could get a job with Roy tomorrow at six quid a week, an' be doin' summat useful.'

'Don't give me that again, Norman Clough. I won't 'ear of it. A lad wi' your brains leavin' school to be a mechanic ! You just stay where you are an' put your back into it, and you'll finish up a scientist. Your form-master told me so 'isself. As promisin' a pupil as 'e's 'ad for years, that's what 'e said.'

'Just butterin' you up,' said Norman. 'Anyroad, what's

wrong wi' bein' a mechanic? You don't see mechanics starvin', any more than scientists. I don't want to mix wi' any o' them fancy folk. I'll stick wi' my own kind an' do t'work I like.'

'Well, you're not leavin' school, an' that's flat.'

'You can't make me stay.'

'Go easy wi' that bowl you're dryin', it cost me six-an'-eleven. No, I can't make you stay, but if you leave it'll be over my dead body, an' Mr Ross's an' all.'

'Corpses everywhere,' said Norman. 'It won't 'alf be a sight!'

'Nay, lad, you're stubborn, like all t'Cloughs. What I'm afraid of is you'll see reason when it's too late. Oh well, let's not go over it again. But I do wish you'd 'ave come with us tonight to meet your cousins. They're takin' a flat in Park Terrace, and your dad an' me are goin' to 'elp wi' t'furniture and make 'em a bit o' supper. I'd like you to come along an' show a bit of interest, like. It's t'lass I'm thinkin' of. There's only 'er and 'er dad – that's my cousin Bob. It'll be right strange for a lass of fifteen who's never been in Yorkshire before an' doesn't know anybody. It'd be only kind if you was to come along an' see 'er.'

'What did you say 'er name was? Summat weird an' wonderful, I know.'

'Amaryllis.'

Norman rolled his eyes.

'Does it cost a shillin' to speak to 'er?' he asked sardonically.

'They call 'er Ril for short,' said Florrie. 'I've never clapped eyes on 'er since she was a right little lass, but I've met 'er dad many a time, an' I can tell you there's nowt stuck-up about 'im.'

'I thought you said she went to a posh school.'

'Well, she used to. She went to Nightingales. That's on t'South Coast. It's progressive as well as posh. They must be so posh they let 'em do what they like. But, anyroad, now she's comin' up 'ere she'll be goin' to 'Allersage Grammar School, same as you.'

'How too too fearfully common,' said Norman, putting on an accent.

'They're not rich, you know. 'Er dad's a sort of school-master for grown-ups. 'E's goin' to run evenin' classes 'ere for West Ridin' University.'

Fred put his head round the door.

'I'm off to t'Feathers,' he said. He looked at Florrie questioningly.

'All right,' said Florrie; and then, after a moment, 'Go on, I'm not stoppin' you.'

Fred disappeared. Florrie sighed.

'There you are, Norman love,' she said. 'That's life with your dad. There's nowt wrong with 'im, mind you. 'E's bin a good 'usband to me an' a good father to you. But what matters in 'is life is 'is allotment an' pigeons an' suppin' pints at t'local wi' t'lads. I'd like you to grow up to summat more interestin' than that.'

'I shall,' said Norman with assurance. 'Dad's old-fashioned, that's all. This is t'nineteen-sixties.'

'I'm not thinkin' of jive an' motor-bikes,' said Florrie. 'There's things that matter more than them.' She was silent for a moment before continuing: 'Now take Cousin Bob. There's a man of ideas. An educated man.'

'You take 'im,' said Norman. ''E doesn't sound like my cup o' tea. 'Ow do we come to 'ave this man of ideas in t'Clough family?'

'Ideas is nowt new in our family,' said Florrie huffily. 'Remember old Caradoc!'

'Oh, don't dig 'im up – t'family skeleton. I've 'eard plenty about 'im. But I'd never 'eard of Cousin Bob till a week or two ago. You never used to talk about 'im.'

'Well, 'e's only a distant relative,' Florrie admitted. ''Is

9

grandpa was first cousin to Great-Aunt Martha. I don't know what that makes 'im. But Cloughs 'as allus stuck together, an' seein' 'e's comin' 'ere to live, I mean to make 'im welcome.'

'And 'is darling daughter,' said Norman. He grinned.

'Well, I've seen a picture of 'er, and she looked a right bonny lass.'

'I know what you're up to,' said Norman. 'You want me to take up wi' these superior folks, don't you? They might persuade me to stay at school till I'm about twenty, an' stop seein' Roy Wentworth, an' wear a white collar, an' get a nice safe job? I can read you like a horror-comic. But it won't work, see.'

'All right, all right,' said Florrie calmly. ''Ave it your own way. I just thought you might 'ave troubled to meet t'lass, that's all.'

'I keep tellin' you, I promised to 'elp Roy. 'Ere, let me finish them pans. Now, don't be cross, love. A promise is a promise, 'ow often 'ave you told me that?'

'Well, go round an' see 'er before long, there's a good lad.'

'I'll go in t'mornin',' said Norman, 'an' that's another promise. But you needn't think I'm goin' to get pally with 'er. I can feel in my bones we won't get on.'

*

A battered saloon car chugged its way over a Yorkshire moor and halted at a road junction.

'Hallersage four miles, Leeds twenty-three,' read Robert Terry from the signpost. 'We're nearly there, Ril. Thank goodness for that.'

'I never thought we'd make it,' said his daughter. 'The furniture van must have got there hours ago. That's what comes of having the kind of old crock that boils on every hill. Poor old Daisy. Some day, when we're rich, let's sell her and buy a real car.'

'Come now,' said Robert, 'you know you couldn't bear to part with Daisy.'

'Well, she tries,' said Ril. 'I admit she tries.'

The ancient car crawled painfully into the Hallersage road, headed east, and picked up speed as the road began to slope downhill. The Pennine summits were behind it now. It rattled over a stretch of moorland where sheep wandered about the road. It passed a cold remote tarn which was Hallersage's reservoir. It crossed the headwaters of a stream, gushing and bouncing over stones. Then the road dipped sharply downward, hugging a hillside. And as the old car rounded a bend the whole landscape opened up, and there below was Hallersage.

Robert Terry drew in to the kerb beside a low stone wall.

'Let's finish that flask of coffee,' he said, 'and you can have your first look at Hell's Edge.'

'Why do they call it Hell's Edge . . .?' began Ril, but as she leaned over the wall and looked at the town below her voice trailed away. The question was answered.

Hallersage filled all the lower end of a pear-shaped valley. Though it was a clear July evening, the town lay under a faint smoky haze. It was an endless grey huddle of houses and factories, tangled tightly together. There were hundreds of chimneys, most of them smoking. Here and there was a church spire. A murky river threaded its way through railway sidings, coal-dumps, warehouses, and the black relics of Victorian industry. There were two open spaces: the football ground and the cemetery.

On the opposite bank of the valley the town continued. Here were mostly houses: crazy terraces that went up and down like rows of steps; houses on a score of different levels and at a score of different angles; houses all blackened and all puffing out more smoke. Finally, far above everything else, small and remote and lonely, was the white cube of a farmhouse, like something left over from another age.

As Ril and her father watched, the sun began to set. Above the grimy basin of the town the sky reddened to a lake of flame.

'What a wonderful sunset!' said Ril.

'Dramatic, isn't it?'

'It really does look like hell's edge!'

' "Hallersage, hell's edge",' quoted Robert. 'That's what they say in other Yorkshire towns. Whatever you do, Ril don't ask the way to the Edge. It's like going to Wigan and asking for the pier. They don't think it's funny.'

Ril sipped her coffee.

'I can't really believe we're going to live down there,' she said. 'Not after Belhampton. Just think of the sea and the Downs and the lovely fresh air.... Oh dear, I'm sorry. I'd better start forgetting it.'

She sat sideways on the wall and said no more.

Robert looked at her with concern. He was a tall thin man with a round spectacled face and an amiable expression. Ril was not particularly like him. Though she did not know it, there was more of the Clough in her; dark curly hair, firm chin, not quite a pretty face, but bright eyes and a clear skin.

Robert sighed. A daughter was a responsibility. It was ten years since Ril's mother had died. The girl was growing up fast. He felt guilty about uprooting her from the South Coast town where she had spent all her life, and still more guilty about taking her away from Nightingales. To be a day-girl with a scholarship at one of the best-known schools in the country – that wasn't an advantage to be thrown away lightly.

On impulse Robert said: 'You could still stay at Nightingales, even now. They won't have filled your place yet. I could find the boarding fees somehow.'

'What, and leave you on your own in a place like this? You'd hate it, Daddy. You know you would. Besides, you'd never get any proper meals or wear a clean shirt.'

'I could manage.'

'There's no need to.'

Robert was silent for a moment. Then:

'I shouldn't have taken the job,' he said.

Ril sighed.

'Of course you should,' she said patiently. 'We talked it over at the time. Now don't start blaming yourself. Let's try and look forward to life in Hallersage, shall we? Tell me about these cousins of ours. I didn't even know we had any until the other day.'

'Well, they're pretty distant cousins,' said Robert. 'They're mostly Cloughs. The Cloughs are my mother's family. They've lived in Hallersage for generations – ever since it was a village. You must have heard me talk about Fred and Florrie. They have a boy, Norman, not much older than you. Then there are the Albert Cloughs down at Lower Mill, and the William Cloughs out on the Leeds Road, but I've rather lost touch with them.'

'And what sort of people are all these Cloughs?'

'Oh, ordinary working folk.'

'No top people?'

'Definitely no top people,' said Robert, smiling.

'I'm disappointed in you. I think we might have had important connexions. Or if it's an ancient family couldn't we have had a famous ancestor or something?'

'Well, as to that,' said Robert thoughtfully, 'you have an ancestor who made his mark, though he wasn't exactly famous. He was transported to Australia.'

'That doesn't sound like anything to boast about.'

'Oh, I don't know. . . . Have you ever heard of Caradoc Clough?'

'No. What a funny name.'

'Yes, it is a funny name. Caradoc of course is Welsh, and Clough is as North Country as they come. I don't think there was anything Welsh about this Caradoc, but . . . oh, it's a long story, Ril. I'll tell you some other time. Tonight, perhaps. We'd better be getting on our way.'

It was dusk now. Robert and his daughter returned to the car. Cautiously, in low gear, Robert followed the steep winding road down into the depths of Hallersage. Ril realized they were passing through the town centre when she saw neon signs and lighted showroom windows, and she could just make out the outline of a huge Gothic town hall. Twice they overtook tramcars, groaning on their way like doomed and bulky monsters.

From the town centre they drove up a long, rising road. 'We're going up the valley now,' said Robert. 'The flat I took is part of a converted house in Old Hallersage. That's the original village – swallowed up by the town now, of course. Fred and Florrie live there, and the grammar school's almost round the corner.'

The car turned into a side-road. It was wide, paved with stone setts. On the left was a tiny park; on the right a row of biggish stone houses with little strips of front garden. All seemed to have been made into flats, and in one of them a first-floor window blazed forth.

'That's us,' said Robert.

'No sign of the furniture van.'

'Maybe Fred and Florrie have coped with it,' said Robert. He fumbled for his keys. Then there was a clatter of descending footsteps, and the door was flung wide by a solid red-faced woman in an apron.

'Welcome to Hallersage!' she cried. 'Welcome home!'

Florrie wiped her hands on her apron, embraced Robert briefly, and clasped Ril to her bosom before pushing her to arm's length in order to see her under the light.

'So this is t'lass,' she said. 'Eh, isn't she like 'er grandma! I'd 'ave known 'er anywhere for a Clough!'

'Ril, this is your Cousin Florrie,' said Robert. 'Let's see, what is it exactly, Florrie? Second cousin, third cousin?'

'Third, once removed, I make it,' said Florrie without hesitation. 'But blood's thicker than water, they say, even at that distance. Eh, I'm right glad to see you. Me an' Fred's bin 'ere since five o'clock. We've seen to your furniture, and there's a right nice 'otpot on t'stove. An' we've bin long enough talkin' on t'step, 'aven't we? Ril love, you're shiverin'. Come inside, both of you, an' get warm.'

*

Only Florrie Clough's idea of a Yorkshire welcome could have led anyone to light a fire on such a mild summer night. But there in the flat was a blazing coal fire, and there too was such of the Terrys' furniture as they had decided to keep when leaving Belhampton. Ril thought it looked odd but reassuring in its new surroundings. She was tired after a long day's travel, and the heat added to her sleepiness. After supper she nodded in an armchair while Florrie talked.

Florrie's talk was unending. She detailed the affairs of numerous members of the family, then moved on to the neighbours. The colour of Great-Aunt Martha's curtains – what Mrs Johns had said to the butcher – old Mr Holroyd's operation – all these were of equal and absorbing interest to her. Robert Terry sat beside his daughter, saying little but listening politely. Fred Clough sat at the other side of her, gazing blankly into the fire. Ril remembered something, stifled a yawn, and sat up straight.

'Tell me about Caradoc Clough,' she said.

Florrie and Fred exchanged glances.

'You don't want to bother wi' all that,' said Fred, speaking for the first time for half an hour.

'It'll do no 'arm,' said Florrie.

'It's all over an' done with,' said Fred with emphasis.

'Well, t'lass is a Clough,' said Florrie. 'You've on'y to look at 'er to see she's a Clough. I don't see why she shouldn't know.'

'It's not a family secret, Fred,' said Robert. 'You can find it all in Langley's *West Riding Social History*.'

'Less said about it t'better,' said Fred in a complaining tone. But he knew he had lost. Florrie was settling comfortably into her chair. To her it was as good as gossip.

'Shall I tell the tale, Florrie?' said Robert. 'You can put me right if need be.'

Florrie nodded.

'Caradoc Clough,' said Robert, 'led a rebellion.'

Fred winced. Ril was surprised.

'A rebellion?' she echoed. 'In England?'

'Only a little one,' said Robert, 'and it only lasted a week. It was early in the last century, before Hallersage became an industrial town. The big landowner in these parts, Sir George Withens, arranged for the enclosure of the old Hallersage Common, and got most of it himself. The villagers were shut out of land they'd always had access to, and lost the right to graze their animals there. It was a big blow to their livelihood.'

'It sounds dreadful. How did he get away with it?'

'Oh, it was all quite legal. It was done under Act of Parliament, and there were commissioners to see that everybody who could prove they had rights on the Common got an allotment of land. But half the villagers couldn't prove they had any rights, anyway, and even those who did get an allotment didn't get enough to be of any use.'

'So they resented it?'

'They did indeed. They thought it was a put-up job. So it was, in a way, though to be fair Sir George Withens's aim was to improve the standard of farming rather than just to grab the land from the people. Anyway, two young men called Caradoc Clough and Frank Thwaite organized a band of people to tear down the fences as soon as they were put up. That led to riots and rick-burning, and a parish constable got a crack on the head. Then the landlords called out the militia – officered by their own friends and relations – and soon put a stop to it all. Clough and Thwaite were tried at Quarter Sessions and sentenced to seven years' transportation.'

'They was lucky not to be 'ung,' interposed Florrie.

'Their efforts didn't do any good,' said Robert. 'In fact Sir George replaced his fences by a high stone wall, so the villagers couldn't even see their Common any more. But Clough wouldn't admit defeat. He stood up in court when sentence was passed and called out something like this: "By force and by fraud you have robbed us of our birthright, but this I declare – that what the folk of Hallersage have lost, the folk of Hallersage shall one day recover." '

'And did they recover it?' asked Ril.

'They did not,' said Robert drily. 'It's Withens land to this day.'

'And t'town could do wi' it, I can tell you,' added Florrie. 'It's at t'top end o' t'valley, above 'ere. There's bin talk from time to time of buyin' it for playin'-fields an' such, but t'Withenses won't part.'

'What happened to Caradoc and his friend?' asked Ril.

'Oh, they served their sentences and came back to Hallersage. Their families had survived somehow. And, as you know, the Cloughs are still here in Hallersage today.'

''E was a character, was old Caradoc,' remarked Florrie, 'from what Great-Aunt Martha says.'

Ril stared.

'You don't mean there's somebody who remembers him?'

'I do that. Aunt Martha remembers 'im as clear as day. Clearer than she remembers what 'appened last week, in fact.'

'But it was all so long ago.'

'The Hallersage Rebellion was in 1825 if my memory's correct,' said Robert.

'That's right,' agreed Florrie. 'But Caradoc was a young

man then. Aunt Martha remembers 'im as an old chap wi' a stick, when she was nobbut a lass.'

'She must be pretty old, even so,' said Ril.

'She's ninety-eight,' said Florrie, slowly and with suitable emphasis. 'And Aunt Martha knows more about t'owd Common than you'll find in any 'istory book.'

'That'll do,' said Fred. He had been scowling into the fire. Now he stood up.

'We don't want to start rakin' up t'past,' he went on. 'What's done is done. And t'Withenses can still be nasty now if they feel like it. So let's drop t'subject, shall we? Now, Bob, what about a pint at t'Feathers afore they close?'

'That's a pleasant thought,' said Robert. 'Florrie, are you going to join us?'

'Nay, if you don't mind, Robert, I won't,' said Florrie comfortably. 'I'll just get t'washin'-up done, an' then 'appen me and 'er ladyship 'ere can unpack some o' them trunks o' yours.'

'Oh, don't bother with that, Cousin Florrie!' said Ril. 'I'll do it myself later on.'

'I'd rather be doin' summat than just sittin' around,' said Florrie, as she collected the plates. 'Eh, love, I do 'ope you'll like it 'ere. It'll seem right strange to you, I shouldn't wonder. 'Allersage ways aren't your ways. Though I must say your dad allus seems quite at 'ome. I'm sorry our Norman isn't 'ere to meet you. 'E says 'e'll come in t'mornin'. If I'd 'ad my way 'e'd 'ave bin 'ere tonight, but these days lads won't do owt if they don't feel like it. 'E's independent, is our Norman.'

'Is he interested in the Caradoc story?' asked Ril.

'Who? Norman?' Florrie shook her head. 'Nay, it's not in 'is line. 'E goes in for mechanical things – car engines an' such. Mind you, 'e's got plenty o' spirit, 'as t'lad, and 'e's adventurous, like. As a matter o' fact, 'is second name's

18

Caradoc – it were Aunt Martha that wanted 'im called that. But 'e 'asn't any time for all that old stuff.'

'Nor has Cousin Fred, has he?'

'Well, Cloughs is workin' folk, love. There's enough to do wi' worryin' about today's troubles, never mind them from t'past. Now, where shall we put these 'ere sheets?'

*

Norman groped for the spanner, found it by touch, and felt it solid in his hand. Lying on his back he could just reach the last nuts to be tightened. Gently he applied pressure: it was no good using brute force, you might break the thread.

That was the end of the job, and the most satisfying moment. He eased himself from under the car. Roy was waiting for him.

'You were long enough over that,' he remarked.

'I made a proper job of it.'

'You'll never learn, will you, lad? What the eye can't see the heart won't grieve at.'

'I made a proper job of it,' Norman repeated.

Roy Wentworth sighed. He was a smart, well-dressed, and good-looking young man in his middle twenties. Car dealing was his business; the garage was a mere shack behind his showrooms where cars were repaired before being sold.

'Don't ask me why I employ you,' he said.

'I don't need to ask you. It's because I'm cheaper than a mechanic an' better than an apprentice, that's why.'

'And you take a lot more time,' said Roy.

There was no heat in the argument. They had been through it all before.

'Anyway, thank God that one's finished,' Roy went on. 'I want to lock up and get away. I'm taking a girl out.'

'Sylvie?'

Roy nodded.

'Someone ought to warn 'er about you,' said Norman.

'She knows all about me. She's mad about me, lad.'

'She's mad, full stop,' said Norman. 'Did you put a new tail-lamp in this car I've bin workin' on?'

'I forgot. Take one out of the Morris over there. It won't be missed – not till he's away from here, anyway.'

'I'll 'ave nowt to do wi' that,' said Norman. 'Do your own dirty work. An' what about givin' me my money?'

'Let's see,' said Roy. 'Three hours at two-and-eight, that's six-and-fourpence. . . .'

He was grinning. He didn't expect to get away with it.

'Three an' a half hours at two-an'-eight,' said Norman, 'is nine-an'-four. Dirt cheap at the price. An' I don't know why you bother to diddle me, considerin' the packet you're makin'.'

'Look after the pence,' said Roy sententiously, 'and the pounds will look after themselves. In fact they do.'

'You're a crook, Roy Wentworth,' said Norman.

'I'm a business man,' said Roy.

'Same thing.'

'Not at all. Business is business.'

'Well, that's one way o' puttin' it. I can think of others. Anyroad, you're welcome to whatever you make like that. I'd rather do a fair day's work for a fair day's pay myself.'

'I expect that's all you'll ever do,' said Roy. 'A pity. You're a bright lad, Norman, but you'll never make your fortune. Anyway, you can come again tomorrow if you like. There's still plenty to do.'

'Tomorrow's Sat'day. I can't come till after dinner. I'm 'elpin' Jim 'Arrison with 'is bike, first thing. Then I've to go an' say 'ullo to my cousin from t'South – just to please my mum, like.'

'What's his name? – the cousin, I mean.'

'It's not a him, it's a her. She's only a distant cousin.'

'Aha. Pretty?'

'My mum says so. But you needn't start gettin' interested. She's only my age.'

'One for you, eh? Time you had a girl-friend, Norman. How old are you – nearly sixteen? You're backward, lad, that's what you are, backward.'

'Aw, give it a rest,' said Norman. 'Don't you ever think of owt but girls an' money?'

'Sometimes,' said Roy. 'If I really have to.'

He was teasing.

'They ought to 'ang a notice on you, "Public Menace",' said Norman. 'Anyroad, you stick to Sylvie. At least that keeps you out o' t'way o' t'rest.'

'What will you do to entertain this cousin of yours?'

'I reckon I needn't do much. Show 'er t'sights, maybe. I might take 'er for a coffee in t'Italia Bar – that's a bit less dead-an'-alive than most of 'Allersage.'

'Maybe I'll see you, then. I'm meeting a customer near there. I might drop into the Italia later on.'

'I can't stop you,' said Norman.

Through a crack in the curtains a thin shaft of sunlight fell on to Ril's pillow. Half awake, she turned over. She had been dreaming of Belhampton, and as the dream faded she tried vainly to hold on to it. She was still there, she pretended, at the house in Bay Road with the Downs above her and the little town and its harbour below. It was a sunny summer morning and she was going for a ramble along the coast with her friend Gillian. They were setting out along Bay Road, they were crossing the stile into the fields, they were walking over the grass with the blue sea far beneath them and the headland hazy in the distance. . . .

But it was no good. Hallersage was breaking into her dream. Hallersage was reality from now on. For a moment, fully awake, she found it hard not to cry.

Still, the sunshine was real. Ril got up. It was half past seven. Drawing the curtain she saw that she was not quite in the depths, for most of Hallersage lay below her. The view was mainly of roof-tops: roof-tops and chimneys and still more chimneys. But beyond them were the hills. And who would have guessed that roof-tops could be so different – so many colours and shapes and sloping so many ways? A black cat picked its delicate way along a parapet; that was for luck. Ril's spirits rose again. It was a bright sunny Saturday morning and here she was fit and well, in a new place with new things to do.

She went to make some tea and found that her father was already up. They had breakfast together at the table in the window of the one living-room. The sun still shone, and from this side of the house they looked out over a park. It was only a tiny park – no more than a token – but it blazed bravely with flowers.

'That's a pint-sized affair, isn't it?' remarked Ril.

'Be thankful for it,' said Robert. 'Land's scarce in Hallersage.'

'Haven't you been clever?' said Ril admiringly. She hadn't really thought her father could be trusted to take a flat. But here they were, quite nicely placed, and it wasn't a bad flat at all. Her eyes wandered round. They had a good-sized living-room, a decent kitchen, two passable bedrooms, a bathroom. It wasn't much, but it was enough, and there was nothing poky about it.

Robert looked complacent. He thought he had been clever, too.

'I'm going to like it here!' Ril declared optimistically.

Then she remembered Belhampton, and again for a moment she could have cried.

'We'll go round to the school on Monday,' said Robert. 'We're going to see Miss Sadler. She's the deputy head. The head's a man. I forget his name, but anyhow he's away in America studying something or other. There's only a couple of days of term to go. I shouldn't think you'll start till autumn.'

'Florrie said my cousin Norman would come round this morning,' said Ril. 'You met him when you were here before, didn't you? What's he like? Shall I like him?'

'I'm not sure,' said Robert thoughtfully. 'He struck me as a decent kind of lad, but he's a pretty rough diamond. I'd better leave you to make up your own mind. What time's he coming?'

'Florrie didn't say.'

'I thought you and I might have gone out, and I'd have shown you round the district. But perhaps you'd better wait for him. Anyway, I've got lots of work to do. I'll have a busy time in the next few weeks, I'm afraid, preparing for the autumn session. Shall I take you round to Florrie's to collect him?'

'Oh no,' said Ril. 'Let him come for me.'

She had plenty to do. There were possessions to be sorted out, and there were things that Florrie had arranged to be rearranged. Ril found out where the stop-tap and the electric meters were, and what kind of fuses were needed, having a shrewd idea that none of these questions would ever occur to her father until there was a crisis.

Meanwhile a fine morning was passing. Ril began to get annoyed with the unknown Norman for not turning up. It was after twelve when the outer doorbell rang. She slipped a cardigan on and ran down the steps, ready to go out.

The boy who confronted her was half a head taller than

she was; he had a bush of black hair and would have looked silly in a school cap. His expression was wary.

'Hullo,' said Ril.

''Ullo.'

'You're Norman.'

'Aye. You're . . .' Norman decided not to attempt the name.

'People call me Ril.'

'Oh aye.' He was silent.

'It's a nice afternoon,' said Ril with an edge of sarcasm.

'You what?'

'I mean,' said Ril patiently, 'that it's after twelve o'clock.' Norman didn't look as if he thought that was funny.

'I've been up since half past seven,' Ril went on.

'I've bin up since that time myself,' said Norman. 'Workin'.'

'Working?'

'On a bike.'

Ril raised her eyebrows questioningly, but Norman offered no more information.

'I'm told I've to show you round 'Allersage,' he said. The tone was faintly hostile.

Ril ignored it and smiled.

'You don't have to do anything,' she said. 'But it's nice to meet you. I did like your mother.'

As she said it Ril realized it wasn't the right thing. Norman looked at her with slight distaste, as if she were some foreign food that he didn't much fancy.

'Well, come on,' he said. 'We'll go down to t'town.'

'I'd be quite happy just to look round Old Hallersage,' said Ril.

'There's nowt in Old 'Allersage.'

'There's the school, isn't there? I'd like just to have a first glimpse.'

'I see enough o' school in t'week,' said Norman, 'wi'out goin' there at weekends an' all.'

'And isn't there the Withens estate? And the moors?'

'All you'll see o' t'Withens estate,' said Norman, 'is a great big wall wi' spikes on top. An' as for t'moors, you can keep 'em. All right for sheep, 'appen, but no use to me.'

'All right, all right,' said Ril. 'We'll go wherever you like.'

They walked as far as the main road and arrived at a tram-stop.

'I'm looking forward to a tram ride,' said Ril. 'It's a new experience. I'd never seen a tram until last night.'

'It's time they scrapped t'things,' said Norman, 'an' got some proper transport.'

'Oh,' said Ril blankly. She knew nothing about the merits of transport systems, but she knew when she was being snubbed. She and Norman looked coldly at each other and there was a heavy silence.

Ril cheered up a little when the tram came swaying down the road, with a clanging of bells and a thin wail of wheels on metal track. She and Norman climbed up a perilous out-side staircase and sat one at each end of a smooth curved bench in the prow of the tram. It lumbered off again, gather-ing pace on the downhill slope into town until it reached its maximum of possibly twenty miles an hour. At this speed it rolled alarmingly, and when, approaching the town centre, it turned abruptly at a right angle, Ril shot along the polished seat and cannoned into Norman. Neither of them laughed.

The main streets of Hallersage were canyons between tall, gloomy Victorian buildings – some with modern shop-fronts slapped on to them at random. Traffic jams were continuous. To Ril's ears, used to the calm of Belhampton, the noise was shattering.

'We'll go an' 'ave a cup o' coffee,' said Norman, announc-ing his programme rather than suggesting it. 'This way – through t'market.'

They walked through a covered market – glass-roofed like a railway station, but brighter and livelier. There were stalls laden with trotters, tripe, cowheels, udders, black-puddings, sheeps' hearts, pigs' cheeks. There were thousands of bales of cloth for sale by the yard. Broad, bustling house-wives jostled and poked and prodded and haggled. A hundred brisk arguments went on in hard, forthright Yorkshire tones.

In the middle of the market was an eating-place, with tables and benches set out clockwise round a central stall, looking rather like a stationary roundabout. Here customers ate hot pies and chips and peas, splashed with vinegar. Norman led the way past it, and also past a pet-stall chirruping with budgies and a bookstand piled high with dog-eared paperbacks. And out they went through the other door of the market and into the next street, where a sign said 'Italia Espresso Bar'.

This was Hallersage's shining example of modernity. There was plate-glass and laminated plastic; there were mock stone walls with paper ivy creeping all over them. Wall-lights peeped from pink shells. A huge mural showed the inside of a night-club, with a band playing and people dancing in evening dress. And, rather spoiling the effect, there was a sullen, sluttish waitress with stringy blonde hair.

There was an awkward silence as Norman and Ril sat opposite each other.

'What form are you in at school?' Ril asked after a minute, by way of making conversation.

'Lower Sixth.'

'What are your subjects?'

'Maths, physics, chemistry.'

'I wish I was some good at those,' said Ril. 'I always remember somebody talking about mathematics as a language.'

A flicker of interest came into Norman's face.

'Aye,' he said. 'It is, sort of. It's a different way o' thinkin'.'

'You're lucky. It doesn't mean a thing to me.'

'Oh, aye, maths is all right. I don't mind t'subjects I'm interested in. It's all the other stuff at school that I get fed up with. You know, the kid stuff. Wearin' a cap on school-days, and playin' daft games, and sittin' through lessons that's never goin' to be any good to me, like English and 'istory.'

'What do you mean, no good to you?' demanded Ril. 'You wouldn't get far without English.'

'I know all of it I need. I can say what I think and I can write what I mean. They can keep the rest. And 'istory, flippin' 'istory. The past. What did t'past ever do for me?'

History was Ril's favourite subject. She bristled.

'The past did everything for you,' she said. 'History's fascinating!'

A look of pure disgust passed over Norman's face. The juke-box in the corner drowned his reply by bursting suddenly into one of the popular songs of the day. Ril knew the tune. Her foot tapped. So did those of the other half-dozen people in the café.

'Oh, there's Roy,' said Norman without any great enthusiasm. 'See 'im? That tall feller over there in t'corner. An' there's Cliff.'

Roy had been watching in a patronizing way as Cliff operated a pin-table. Now he signalled to Norman and strolled across, smiling his attractive smile and flicking an imaginary speck from his Continentally cut suit.

'Introduce me to the young lady, Norman,' he said, half bowing.

'My cousin Ril,' said Norman shortly. 'Roy. Cliff.'

'And a very charming cousin,' said Roy.

'Usin' t'showroom accent today, Roy, eh?' said Norman. 'Very smooth, too. Congratulations.'

Roy ignored him. 'Say something to the lady, Cliff,' he continued.

Cliff blushed and mumbled something. He was a cheerful round-faced lad of fifteen, untidy and boyish. Ril didn't know quite what to make of Roy, but thought that Cliff was rather nice.

'You must forgive them their lack of manners,' said Roy. 'They're only schoolboys after all.'

'Well, I'm a schoolgirl,' said Ril.

'No one would think so,' said Roy, with the air of one delivering a compliment. 'Cigarette?'

'No, thank you, I don't.'

'How wise you are,' said Roy. He took a cigarette from a handsome case and lit it with a handsome lighter. The juke-box fell silent for a moment, then broke into another tune.

Ril sipped her coffee. To her surprise it was excellent.

'And how do you like Hallersage, Miss – er . . . ?' began Roy in a courtly tone.

'Come off it, Roy!' said Norman. ''Er name's Ril, and she's only human. At least, I suppose she's only human.'

'Ril,' mused Roy. 'Ril. Now I wonder what that would be short for.'

'Amaryllis.'

Cliff spluttered. He thought it was funny. Norman looked embarrassed, as if his companion had claimed to be Marie Antoinette.

'Amaryllis,' echoed Roy. He said it again, rolling it round his tongue. 'Amaryllis. A delightful name. I shall call you that, if I may.'

'I think it's a bit much for everyday use,' said Ril. 'It appealed to my parents. I don't know whether I like it or not – I'm just used to it.'

'I think it's a daft name,' said Norman.

'Your cousin has no poetry in him,' said Roy. 'Now I –'

'Aw, stuff it, Roy!' muttered Norman. 'Anyway, come on, Ril, I'm supposed to be showin' you round town.' He drained his cup and moved to go.

'A conducted tour?' inquired Roy. 'Can I help? I have a vehicle outside. One of the new Triumphs, actually.'

'Oh, do you have a Triumph?' asked Ril with interest.

'If I was you,' said Norman grimly, 'I'd keep away from 'im. *And* 'is Triumph.'

'Come, come, Norman,' said Roy, unperturbed, but Norman had taken Ril's arm and was leading her outside.

'Look here!' said Ril crossly when they were in the street. 'I can take care of myself, thank you. And you didn't have to be so rude!'

'Can't you see he was only playin' you up?' demanded Norman. ''E doesn't talk that fancy way as a rule, I can tell you. 'E thought it'd go down well wi' you, and I expect 'e was right.'

'At least he was polite,' said Ril.

'Polite!' echoed Norman. He faced her angrily.

'I'm not good enough for you, am I?' he demanded. 'That's what's at t'bottom of it. You with your lah-di-dah ways and your history-is-fascinating and all that. You can't stand a bit o' plain Yorkshire speech.'

'You had that in your head before you ever met me,' said Ril. 'I don't care tuppence how you speak. I like people for what they are, not for what they sound like.'

'That's what you say,' said Norman. His anger was turning to gloom. 'Anyroad, I bet you won't go anywhere wi' me again, will you? I can always tell when people hit it off, and we don't.'

Ril put out her hand. 'I don't see why we shouldn't get on together,' she said. 'Let's not fall out as soon as we've met.'

'Still, you wouldn't go out wi' me, would you?' he persisted.

'Of course I would.'

'I bet you wouldn't go to t'Saturday hop at t'Rex ballroom!'

Ril had no idea what kind of event this might be, but felt it would not do to hesitate.

'I'd love to,' she said.

Norman brightened.

'All right, we'll go next week,' he said. 'Now I'd better get on with showin' you round. This big black buildin' we're just passin', wi' lots of turrets an' twiddles, is 'Allersage Town 'All. And next to it, that's t'Law Courts. . .'

*

'Well, 'ow did you get on wi' your cousin?' demanded Florrie.

Norman turned over a page of *The Autocar*.

'Oh, all right,' he said.

'She's a right nice lass, i'n't she?' Florrie went on. 'I've quite took to 'er, I 'ave that.'

''Ave you?'

'Nice lookin' an' all.'

'Is she?'

'Well, you've got eyes in your 'ead, 'aven't you? Don't tell me you didn't notice.'

'Oh aye, she's all right. But you should 'ear t'things she talks about. " 'Istory is fascinatin'," she says to me. 'Istory! An' when we gets to t'old Assembly Rooms she starts imaginin' folks arrivin' in carriages in fancy dress, an' all kinds o' stuff like that, all out of 'er own 'ead. An' then she gets on to me about Caradoc Clough an' that lot, an' there she is in t'middle of 'Allersage 'Igh Street spoutin' speeches about robbin' us of our birthright or summat. I never 'eard owt like it.'

'Ah,' said Florrie. 'That's like 'er dad. They 'ave ideas, these folks. Imagination, like. When you an' me's thinkin' about peelin' t'taties or puttin' a shelf up, their minds is on 'igher things.'

'Meanwhile,' said Norman, 'they've no spuds for dinner an' no shelf to put t'pans on.'

'I reckon,' said Florrie seriously, 'I reckon it's a right privilege to 'ave 'em in t'family.'

'Get away wi' you!' said Norman. 'We're as good as they are any day. Oh, an' to listen to 'er voice, honestly, it puts years on me. Like one o' them young lady announcers on t'telly.'

Norman fell silent. He turned over several pages of *The Autocar* unread. Since the previous day he had been thinking about Ril more than he wanted to, and always with mixed feelings. She had puzzled him and made him impatient, but each time her mind took a different turning from his he had felt a curious impulse to go along with it. Now he scowled and turned over some more pages.

'She's not like us,' he said, 'an' never will be.'

Only Florrie could have detected the faintly rueful note in his voice.

'Norman Clough!' she declared. ''Ere, look at me! You're quite taken wi' yon lass yourself, aren't you?'

Norman closed his magazine.

'I've nowt agen 'er,' he said roughly. 'An' now give it a rest, will you? I'm goin' round to t'garage.'

*

'I expect we'll get used to it,' said Ril, and sighed.

Jane Sadler smiled faintly. She was deputy head of Hallersage Grammar School: a well-groomed woman in her late forties. She had just asked Ril how she liked the North of England.

'You'll find Hallersage Grammar School rather different from Nightingales,' she said.

Ril sighed again.

'All the time I was there,' she said, 'I never realized how nice they were. And now I realize, but it's too late.'

'Not to worry,' said Miss Sadler briskly. 'We're not absolute monsters here, as a matter of fact.'

'Well, of course not. But it's a bit regimented here, isn't it? My cousin told me you have uniforms and school rules and compulsory games and all that.'

'That's not unusual. Though I don't suppose you had many rules at Nightingales.'

'No. They just expected us to behave ourselves. And they didn't bother much about marks and exams and things, but if there was something you got really interested in they'd spend any amount of time helping you. And you could wear what you liked. And they didn't bother you about playing games if you didn't want to. I can swim well and I can sail a boat, but I can't do anything where you have to keep the score.'

'Hm,' said Miss Sadler. 'You're used to doing what you like, and learning for the fun of it – not always competing with people.'

'Yes.'

'Well, it's true that we can't manage it like that. We have plenty of pupils who only work because we make them, or to pass exams. I suppose their background is very different from those of pupils at Nightingales. And life is fairly earnest in Hallersage. Not that we're necessarily any the worse for it.'

'It's all rather grim-seeming,' said Ril, and sighed a third time.

'You'll settle down quite happily,' said Miss Sadler. 'Make up your mind that you like Hallersage. Tell yourself there's nowhere else you'd rather be. At least your father said you have family connexions here – that's something.'

'Yes, I've a sort of cousin at this school. Norman Clough.'

'I know him. A fine lad.'

'But he's so rough. And he doesn't know anything.'

'You mean he doesn't know anything about the things you're interested in. How much do you know about the things he's interested in?'

'He isn't interested in anything except physics and maths and engineering. . . .'

'And don't those count?' asked Miss Sadler.

Ril reddened.

Miss Sadler smiled.

'Your father will be getting tired of waiting,' she said. 'You'd better go to him now. We shall look forward to seeing you next term. You may have something to teach us – and maybe even something to learn. Why don't you come in for Speech Day with your father tomorrow? – it'll give you a glimpse of how we do things.'

Robert Terry was waiting in the adjoining room, talking to the school secretary. He and Ril went down the main staircase into the forecourt, which in fact was no more than a yard, for the school – a tallish Victorian building – was squashed into a narrow site near the old market-place. As they stepped into the sunshine a group of girls went out through the gateway swinging tennis-racquets.

'I've just been hearing about the difficulties they have over games,' said Robert. 'There aren't even any tennis-courts – they go to the public courts down the road. And for most games they have to go right across the town to Leeds Road – half an hour on the tram.'

'Well, the tram's fun,' said Ril. 'It's the only thing about Hallersage that appeals to me so far.'

'It won't appeal so much after a few months of travelling all that distance twice a week.'

'I don't see why they can't get playing-fields near here,' said Ril. 'The town itself is pretty jam-packed, but up here around Old Hallersage it still seems fairly open country.'

'That's an aspect of what we were talking about the other night,' said Robert. 'It's all Withens land, and I don't suppose Miss Withens will let it go. I'll tell you what, Ril, let's walk farther out of town and I'll show you how it all lies.'

*

Robert and his daughter went out through the school gate and crossed the market-place, which was the centre of Old Hallersage and was also the tram terminus. Here could be seen the traces of a submerged village: a few four-square Georgian stone houses, a row of cottages with fanlights, a cluster of stabling now turned into garages or workshops. But it was not easy to pick the old village out, because later builders had filled in every square inch, and this was now just an outlying part of the industrial town of Hallersage.

'That's Florrie's house over there,' said Robert. He pointed to a grey stone cottage, distinguished from its neighbours by gleaming paintwork and a spotlessly scoured step. 'We'll call on her one day soon, but not now.'

Beyond the market-place the road began to wind uphill. On one side the buildings thinned out until there was only a single row of houses and finally nothing at all except the steep rise of the moors. On the other side was a tall stone wall: not drystone, like most of the walls in those parts, but smooth and cemented and crowned with spikes.

Ril remembered what Norman had told her.

'That must be the Withens wall,' she said.

'Yes, indeed,' said Robert, 'and hardly a soul in Hallersage except the tradesmen has ever been inside. An aloof family, the Withenses – and as hard as that wall, they say around here. Miss Withens is the last of them.'

'An aged crone of about eighty, I suppose?' asked Ril.

'Heavens, no,' said Robert. 'I doubt whether Celia Withens is thirty yet. She's supposed to be a great beauty. I've seen her picture in the papers. She's hardly ever in Hallersage. Spends most of her life on the Riviera, I believe.'

The road had narrowed and steepened. Now, so far as the public were concerned, it came to a stop; for it turned abruptly into the Withens estate, and the way was barred by a huge wrought-iron gate. Over the gate was a

34

coat of arms with the motto: 'QUOD TENEO TENEBO'.

'What I have I hold,' Robert translated.

'That sounds tough,' commented Ril.

'It's tough all right,' said Robert, 'and they live up to it. They never yield an inch.'

Outside the wall, the line of the road was continued by a footpath leading up the valley. Robert and his daughter soon left the path and scrambled straight up the hillside, over springy turf and heather. The sun was warm, birds sang, sheep bleated. Ril felt as if she was miles from any-where, and it was a shock to turn round after a few minutes and see all Hallersage extending down the lower part of the valley.

The Withens estate was immediately beneath her, its out-line marked by that formidable wall. Ril was surprised by the extent of it. Most of the Withens land was quite flat and green, and through it ran the river, clear and glinting in the sunshine. A little to the east of it was Old Hallersage. Ril had some difficulty in picking out the grammar school at first; from here it was no more than a little grey cube.

Then, beyond Old Hallersage market-place, the real town began: there were the smoky rows of houses, the first of the factories, the scores of chimney-fingers, the railway sidings. The valley widened to a basin, the river – lost to view for most of its course – emerged again, but by now it was no more than a black thread through a black industrial land-scape.

'The valley goes through a rake's progress, doesn't it?' said Robert. 'So green and rural at the top end, so dirty and urban lower down.'

'The Withenses have the best of it,' said Ril. 'What a shame that the school hasn't any land when they have so much.'

'Such is life,' said Robert.

Ril began to grow indignant.

'Just think!' she said. 'All that for one woman – and a woman who spends her life on the Riviera – while the school-children have to travel for half an hour to get to their play-ing-fields.'

She struck an attitude.

'And not just any schoolchildren,' she went on. 'Your own daughter, too. Your nearest and dearest, condemned to waste the precious hours of her youth . . .'

Robert smiled. Ril had been subdued since arriving in Hallersage. He hoped she was recovering some of her high spirits. 'Quiet, Caradoc!' he said.

At the mention of Caradoc a new thought entered Ril's mind.

'Hey!' she cried. 'Where exactly was the land that Sir George Withens enclosed?'

'To the best of my knowledge and belief,' said Robert, 'it was the stretch we've just been looking at, down there by the river.'

He looked at her mischievously.

'Ideal for playing-fields,' he added.

By tradition the last day of the school year was Speech Day at Hallersage Grammar School. Robert Terry and his daughter were shown to their seats by Hilda Woodward, a thin plain girl with spectacles who had been given a special dispensation to look after them instead of sitting with her form. There was a wait of some minutes, with much fidgeting and chattering among pupils and shushing by the staff. Then the school governors appeared through a side door and took their places on the dais.

Ril watched them one by one as they came in, and thought them rather ordinary-looking. Nearly all were men: some tall, some short, some with spectacles, some going bald, all looking important. There was one iron-haired, iron-faced lady. And then, when all had been seated for a minute or two, there was a shock as the last of the governors entered. The men rose to their feet, cleared their throats, straightened their ties, and smiled ingratiatingly. The last of the governors, cool as an iceberg, nodded round the half-circle of her colleagues and unhurriedly took her seat. Half the school gasped, and from the masculine end of the sixth form came something that sounded suspiciously like a wolf-whistle. For the last of the governors was a superbly attractive young woman.

'It's Miss Withens!' breathed Hilda. 'She hasn't been here for years!'

Miss Withens was unconcerned about the sensation she was making. She crossed her perfect legs, leaned towards the grey-haired lady, and made some remark at which they both smiled. She was blonde, and the shoulders and arms exposed by an un-school-like summer dress were tanned golden.

Ril was dumbfounded. It seemed impossible that this lovely creature could be the representative of the hard and grasping Withens family.

Now the governors stood again, and this time the whole school as well, while Miss Sadler as acting head made her separate entry with the chairman of the governors. The school song was sung, with much moving of lips but a modest volume of sound. The chairman, affable and confident, took the centre of the stage, and the other governors settled down into their seats.

Ril transferred her attention from Miss Withens to the chairman, who was almost as striking a figure in a different way. He was red-faced and heavy-jowled, with thinning grey hair. His expensive suit was slightly crumpled. He was about average height, but a prominent stomach made him seem shorter. His voice was loud and his accent assertively Northern. And he was enjoying himself.

'It's always a pleasure for me,' he began, 'as a lad who left school at twelve, to come here among all these highly educated colleagues, and to look at you lads and lasses all getting a splendid education at the public expense – and good luck to you, I may say, for I'd be the last to grudge it – and to think how you'll all be spared the struggles that men of my generation have struggled to spare you.

'Now when I left school what were my prospects? I'll tell you. A job in the mill at a few shillings a week – less than most of you get for pocket-money. And nothing to look forward to but a life of toil. But there were some of us who rose above it, all the same. Oh yes, there's much you could teach me, even the smallest of you here today, about languages and such, but I venture to say'– here he made a pause for effect – 'I venture to say that there's just a little that a practical chap like myself can teach the educated folks like you.'

'Hear, hear,' said a bored voice from among the governors.

'Who is it?' Ril whispered to Hilda. 'The speaker, I mean.'

'That's Sam Thwaite,' said Hilda. 'Alderman Thwaite.'

'How did he come to be chairman of the governors?'

'Well, he owns half Hallersage.'

'I thought Miss Withens owned half Hallersage.'

'She owns the other half.'

'He lays it on a bit thick, doesn't he?' said Ril. 'All this barefoot-boy stuff, I mean.'

'Now you're being sniffy,' said Hilda. 'It's all quite genuine. He came up the hard way, and he's proud of it, and why not?'

Somebody was shushing them from behind. They shushed. Ril had lost the thread of Mr Thwaite's remarks, and was conscious only that he went on for a considerable time. He was succeeded by a long-drawn-out prize-giving of which the only interesting feature was a series of awards to Hilda. As the procession of ever smaller boys and girls filed up to the platform to receive the ritual handshake and congratulation, Ril's attention wandered back to Miss Withens. Celia Withens sat looking cool and beautiful and quite expressionless: not so much bored as remote. She seemed so out of place, so exotic among her drab middle-aged colleagues, that Ril felt a poem forming in her head. Writing poems was an old hobby, laid aside since her arrival in Hallersage. She took out a pencil and began to scribble:

> 'Among these stone-grey northern unpeople
> She blossoms, a passionflower, daybrightlong...'

'What are you doing?' whispered Hilda.

'Writing a poem.'

'Can I look?'

Ril passed it over. Hilda wrinkled her brows.

'What's it all about?'

'It's about Miss Withens at the prize-giving.'

'It doesn't mean a thing to me.'

Ril was nettled.

'I don't suppose you've heard of modern poetry in Hallersage,' she said. 'Lots of us wrote it at Nightingales.'

Hilda put out her tongue. Somebody shushed them again. Ril realized that the proceedings were drawing to an end. The school song had a second innings, much brisker than the first. The governors, led by the chairman and the acting head, moved in procession down the aisle, and this gave Ril the chance of another look at Miss Withens, walking beside the iron-haired lady and wearing the same aloof and unselfconscious expression as before. And then, after a suitable interval, the whole school scrambled for the doorway and six weeks of freedom.

One of the mistresses touched Robert's sleeve and asked

him to take tea with the governors in the library. Ril could have gone too, but declined and went out through the main entrance with Hilda. In the forecourt stood a row of cars.

'The governors' cars,' said Hilda.

'I suppose they're all at tea.'

'That's it,' said Hilda. 'Not a proper tea, you know – just a little fancy afternoon tea. "Oh, do have an éclair, Mr Thwaite" – that kind of thing.'

'That's a super red Jaguar over there,' said Ril. 'I bet it's Miss Withens's.'

'Could be,' said Hilda. 'The Bentley's Sir William Whitby's. The Rover is Dr. Price's, I think. And the Austin Seven is Miss Murray's – that's the grey-haired lady.'

'Whose is the Rolls?' Ril asked.

It was rather a splendid Rolls: twenty years old if it was a day, but four-square and spotless and gleaming. A chauffeur was flicking its immaculate surface with a duster.

'That's our Sam's,' said Hilda. 'Mr Thwaite's.'

'Very nice too,' said Ril, 'but I fancy the Jag myself. I'm going over to have a look at it.'

'You can't just now. We're not allowed in the forecourt on Speech Day.'

'Well, nobody's told me that officially. Anyway, I'm not in uniform. I shan't be noticed.'

Ril sauntered over to the row of cars and inspected the Jaguar. She was not mechanically minded, but was interested in the speed and appearance of cars. It was the latest open sports model. She contrasted it ruefully with poor old Daisy.

She was leaning over to get a better view of the controls when she realized that someone was standing at her shoulder.

'Don't mind me, just carry on,' said a clear feminine voice.

Ril straightened up. There was Miss Withens. Miss Sadler was with her.

'Oh, it's Amaryllis,' said Miss Sadler, 'and she shouldn't really be here. This is our newest pupil, Miss Withens. She's just come to us from Nightingales.'

'Oh?' said Miss Withens. 'The progressive school? Well, they seem to have taught her a progressive attitude to other people's property. I wonder if she'd like to find me snooping round her bicycle like that.'

She didn't sound cross; only chilly.

Ril looked into her eyes, which were a beautiful clear blue, but distant. It wouldn't be easy to get close to Celia Withens, she thought.

'I'm sorry, Miss Withens,' she said humbly.

'Run along now, Ril,' said Miss Sadler; and, turning to Miss Withens, she went on :

'Well, it's been nice to see you. I'm sorry you couldn't stay to tea. It's so rarely you're in Hallersage . . .'

Ril moved away, but went no farther than the other side of the Rolls, where the chauffeur was now having a rest and a smoke. He was a wizened, greying little fellow, and he gave her a huge wink.

'She's a tough 'un, that Withens lass,' he said. 'But she's a bit of all right to look at, isn't she? Makes me feel young again. . . .'

He and Ril watched from round the bonnet of the Rolls as Miss Withens slid into the driving seat of her car. There came the low exciting note of a sports-car engine revving up, and then she was away.

'It's a lovely car, isn't it, the Jag?' said Ril. 'Don't you wish you were driving that?'

'Nay, I'd as soon stick to t'Rolls,' said the chauffeur. 'A staid old lady, but she'll do for me.'

'It's Alderman Thwaite's Rolls, isn't it?'

'Aye, it's Sam's,' said the chauffeur. 'Here he comes now. Well, Sam, enjoyed thi tea?'

'Nay, Ben, I've had nobbut a quick sup. It's not in my

41

line, yon fancy stuff.' Sam Thwaite spoke more broadly than in the assembly hall. Then he turned to Ril.

'Well, young lady, what can I do for you? Wantin' a lift? We're goin' down into Hallersage.'

An idea was forming in Ril's mind.

'Yes, please, Mr Thwaite,' she said.

''Op in, then. Close t'door. Nay, let me do it. Like this, see. A'right, Ben lad, off we go.'

Silent and stately, the Rolls sailed out through the main gate. Hilda was just going out. Ril signalled to her and gave a thumbs-up sign.

'Where d'you want to be, lass?' asked Sam Thwaite.

'I was going to the public library, Mr Thwaite.'

'We can drop you at t'door. . . . You don't come from these parts, do you?'

'I'd never been here until the other day,' said Ril. 'But I come from an old Hallersage family.'

'Oh? And who are they?'

'The Cloughs.'

'Now, let's see. Fred Clough? Albert Clough?'

'Fred Clough's a sort of cousin.'

'Oh, I know Fred Clough well,' said Mr Thwaite. 'Him an' me were at school together, at t'owd Lower Mill board school. Aye, I've been in many a scrape wi' Fred. I don't see much of 'im now, mind. I took t'high road and he took t'low road, you might say. But he's a good lad. I'd sup a pint wi' Fred Clough any day o' t'week. Where are you living, lass?'

'With my father. We have a flat at 5, Park Terrace.'

'Oh aye? That's Withens property.'

'Is it?' said Ril. 'Somebody told me today that Miss Withens owns half Hallersage and you own the other half.'

'Well, not quite that,' said Sam Thwaite. 'I 'ave a tidy bit o' property, it's true. Property's my business, you know.

But t'Withenses are t'real landlords round 'ere. Thousands of acres, and they never let go of an inch. And Celia Withens is a right chip off the old block.'

'Yet she looks so lovely,' said Ril.

'Aye, she does that. Well, appearances are deceptive, they say. Mind you, I don't know what yon Celia might be like if you got to know 'er well. She isn't easy to know. We 'ave to judge 'er by 'er actions, an' there's no doubt about it, she's 'ard.'

'I gather she isn't often in Hallersage.'

'No. Spends most of 'er time in t'South o' France. Matter o' fact, I believe things 'aven't been too good for 'er just lately. Doc Price tells me she 'ad an un'appy love affair. So she's come 'ere to lick 'er wounds, I daresay. And do a bit o' business, of course. She leaves most of it to old Tom Cassell, her lawyer, but there's allus lots o' business pilin' up with an estate that size.'

'Do you know anything about Caradoc Clough?' asked Ril suddenly.

Sam Thwaite shot her a sharp glance. Until that moment he had merely been chatting. Now he was alert.

'I've 'eard of 'im,' he said warily. 'What do *you* know?'

'Not much,' Ril admitted. 'But I'm interested in finding out.'

'Curiosity killed the cat,' said Sam Thwaite.

Ril stared at him.

'Nay, don't be alarmed,' said Sam. 'I only mean that in this town it isn't a good idea to get across the Withens family. Some folks 'ave done, and the Withenses made it very nasty for 'em. They 'ave influence in 'igh places, you know.'

'What makes you think I'd get across them?'

'Well, if you're interested in Caradoc Clough I'd like to bet there's a motive behind it,' said Sam. 'There's some as say the old Common could be got back for Hallersage if everyone knew their rights. But I doubt it. Nay, I don't want to discourage you. You're a bright lass, I can see that. But I'm just tellin' you, watch your step.'

'Everyone tells me that Hallersage is crying out for land,' said Ril.

'It is that.'

'And Miss Withens has all those acres. Can't they *make* her give some of it up?'

'Compulsory purchase, you mean? Not a hope, lass. T'Corporation'll buy it all right, but she'll have to agree to sell.'

'And won't she?'

'Not so far. We've tried two or three times. I reckon she'll part wi' it in t'long run, but not yet awhile, unless summat 'appens to shake 'er. T'Withenses take some shiftin'.'

Sam Thwaite sighed.

'There, now,' he said, 'we're just comin' up to t'public library.'

'I suppose they'll have a copy of Langley's *Social History*?' said Ril.

'Oh aye,' said Sam. 'Oh aye. And – here, lass, you can come and see me some day and tell me 'ow you've got on. T'address is on this card.'

'Thank you, Mr Thwaite,' said Ril. 'I will. And thank you for the lift.'

Ril was turning away from the car to go into the public library when Sam tapped at the window.

' 'Ere,' he said. 'Next time you go to your Cousin Fred's tell 'em you want to talk to t'owd lady. See what you can learn from 'er.'

*

It was hot, that last week in July. Hallersage sweltered in its basin-like valley. Norman was working each day at Roy Wentworth's garage, earning money with which he planned to buy a motor-bike. In three months' time he would be sixteen: old enough to hold a licence. Robert Terry was also busy, drawing up programmes and preparing lectures for the autumn session. Only Ril had time to spare. She had always been a reader, but in the long summer days books were not company enough. She wanted somebody to saunter round and talk and laugh with: a girl-friend in fact. On Speech Day she had suggested that Hilda Woodward should come round, but Hilda had not appeared and Ril did not know her address.

Twice Ril took herself to the public baths, but they were enclosed and crowded and the water tasted of chlorine. She walked on the moors, but they seemed lonely and foreign. When she looked down again on Hallersage from above the drama of her first impression had faded, and the town now seemed unbearably squalid.

Try as she might to avoid it, the homesickness for Belhampton crept over her. She thought about swimming in the sea, about the cliff walks, about the view from her window over Belhampton Bay, and most of all about the friends she had left behind. To revive her interest in Hallersage she read and re-read the pages in Langley's *West Riding Social History* about the Hallersage Rebels. According to Langley, Sir George in his old age was believed to have regretted the enclosure of the Common and to have promised to restore the rights of the townsfolk. But no more was heard of it, and his will left everything to his heirs. Apart from this crumb of information, Langley added little to what Ril already knew. And as she went over it again in the close type of the musty volume the episode seemed faint and far away.

Friday, the third day after Speech Day, was the hottest day so far, and in the evening the heat still lingered oppressively. After supper Ril went down and sat on the doorstep with a book. From the main road thirty yards away came the sounds of traffic; just here the heavy lorries always changed gear as they ground their way out of town. The smell of diesel oil hung on the windless air. In the tiny park opposite, the grass was parched and brown. Ril felt her distaste for Hallersage rising to a head.

Then she remembered Miss Sadler's advice: 'Make up your mind that you like it. Tell yourself there's nowhere else you'd rather be.' She decided to give it a try.

Spoken to herself, the words seemed meaningless. Ril wondered if it would be more effective to say them aloud.

'I like Hallersage,' she said clearly.

An old woman passing by looked at her suspiciously. Ril allowed her to get out of earshot.

'I like Hallersage,' she said again. 'There is nowhere else I would wish to be.'

The image of Belhampton's little fishing harbour, with its score of boats riding at anchor, rose before her eyes. She dismissed it.

'This is the only place for me,' she said. For a moment the sound of her own voice seemed to carry conviction, and she went on:

'Oh, how I do like Hallersage!'

'I'm delighted to hear it,' said a masculine voice.

Ril looked up in embarrassment.

The young man who had emerged from the hallway behind her was in his middle twenties: large, solid, and somewhat rugged-looking. His smile was friendly.

'I'm a neighbour of yours,' he went on. 'I live in the flat above you. My name's James Willoughby, and I work for the Corporation. Now you must be . . .'

'Amaryllis Terry. Please call me Ril.'

'Please call me James.'

'I must have sounded terribly silly, talking to myself.'

'Not at all,' said James. 'It was a joy to hear you. I wish more people felt as you do about Hallersage.'

'But —'

'After all, it is the only place to live. I'm not saying that

46

just because I work for the Corporation. Hallersage is strong, it's full of character, it's even beautiful when you get to know it.'

'But –'

'But it's not often people take to it as quickly as you've done.'

'Well, to tell you the truth . . .' began Ril awkwardly; and as she spoke she heard her father's footsteps on the stairs. Thankful for the interruption, she introduced James to him.

'I was just congratulating your daughter on her taste,' James remarked. 'She likes Hallersage already.'

Robert's eyebrows rose. He looked quizzically at his daughter. Ril said nothing.

'It's music in my ears,' James went on. 'Oh, I know there's a lot wrong with the town – that's why we formed the New Hallersage Society. But even as it is it's a fine town. We shouldn't take it at other people's valuation as an ugly dump.'

'What is the New Hallersage Society?' inquired Robert.

'It's something I hope to interest you in. It's . . . Well, I'd better not try to explain it just now. I must dash off. I'm supposed to be meeting somebody five minutes ago.'

'Well, well,' said Robert as James disappeared. 'An enthusiast!'

'I think he's nice,' said Ril. 'I was surprised when he said he worked for the Corporation. I mean, he doesn't seem the type to be emptying dustbins or digging holes in the road.'

'He has the physique for it,' said Robert. 'However there are other ways of working for the Corporation. I think I heard he was in the legal department. But, Ril, tell me about your conversion to being a lover of Hallersage.'

There was a hopeful note in Robert's voice. Ril did not like to disillusion him. She knew he wanted her to be happy in her new surroundings.

'Well, I suppose it grows on you,' she said heroically.

'That's the spirit. And it's good to meet someone who really loves the place, isn't it?'

To her surprise Ril realized that the encounter with James had cheered her up.

'All the same,' she said to herself, remembering his words, 'it *is* an ugly dump.' And at bedtime she opened her window and confided the message to the roof-tops.

'Hallersage,' she said clearly, 'you are an ugly dump. Do you hear me? An ugly dump.'

All over Hallersage, after Saturday tea, young people got ready for their evening out. Norman spent more than an hour preparing to take Ril to the Rex ballroom. He scrubbed his face, ears, and neck until the skin glowed pink. He astonished Florrie by the attention paid to his fingernails. He borrowed Fred's razor and shaved for the first time in his life, painfully but without injury. He tried in vain to tame his hair. He put on a clean shirt and his best, newly pressed suit. He knotted and re-knotted his tie.

All the time he told himself it wasn't worth it. He wasn't sure that he liked the girl. Perhaps she would be haughty and make him feel small. Perhaps she wouldn't look as nice as he expected. Perhaps she would have forgotten the date, or changed her mind, or her father wouldn't let her come. He was half eager, half nervous, as he approached 5, Park Terrace.

None of his fears was justified. Ril hadn't forgotten. She came to the door, looking livelier and prettier than he'd remembered, and she wasn't a bit haughty. Robert was friendly, too.

'Bring her back by ten-thirty, as good as new,' was his only stipulation. Norman promised earnestly that he would. In a surprisingly short time they were walking along the street together.

For a few minutes there was silence. Conversation was not Norman's strong point. Ril tried to think of something that would interest him.

'Did you see that super red Jag at the school on Speech Day?' she asked. 'It belongs to Miss Withens.'

'Aye, I saw it. I saw 'er, too. But they're too fancy for me, both 'er and t'Jag. I'm savin' up for a motor-bike, though. That's why I keep on workin' for Roy.'

'Can you ride one?'

'Well, I'm not supposed to, but I can. I'll be able to 'ave a licence in September. I've got my eye on an old BSA, 500 c.c. I can get it for next to nowt, but it wants a lot o' work doin' on it.'

'And can you do it?'

'I can that,' said Norman with emphasis. 'There's not much I can't do with engines. I'd get a job tomorrow if I was to leave school.'

'But you wouldn't want to, would you?'

'My mum'd go through t'roof.'

'But even if she agreed?'

'I'm not sure. I might.'

'Well, you'd be silly. I mean, even apart from the interest of what you're doing at school, there'd be a much better job at the end of it.'

Norman was irritated.

'Aw, that sort of talk makes me mad,' he said. 'You're just like my mum and dad. All they can think about is for me to get a fancy job, an' be paid a salary instead o' wages. Well, I'm not interested, see. I'm 'avin' nowt to do wi' t'rat-race.'

Ril had no time to think of an answer because they were

arriving at the Rex. It was a bit of a dump, she thought: a typical back-street dance-hall, with lots of electric lights and neon signs, but seediness showing through. She refrained from comment, but Norman himself seemed to feel that some explanation was needed.

'I thought I'd show you a bit o' t'real 'Allersage,' he said. 'You'll 'ave to take us as you find us 'ere, you know. I daresay it's a change for you. I suppose you're used to 'Unt Balls an' so on.'

Ril smiled at the idea.

'I've never been to anything like that,' she said.

'But you don't care for t'Rex?'

'I don't really know yet.'

'All right, then, come on in.'

With a week's money in his pocket Norman insisted on paying. Inside it was clear that the evening had not yet warmed up. Only a few couples were dancing. Boys and girls were clustered in separate groups round the walls, but there were plenty of empty chairs. The bar – selling soft drinks and ices only – was doing a fair trade. Nobody in the hall appeared to be much over twenty.

Those who danced were all jiving. Ril danced well, and after a dull week she felt vitality bubbling up inside her. As a partner, Norman was slightly disappointing. He was a dogged rather than a natural dancer. Still it was nice to be out on the dance-floor, and she was ready to enjoy herself.

After the second dance someone hailed them from the bar. In that corner of the hall there were a few tables, and Roy and Cliff were sitting at one of them with two girls. Norman and Ril threaded their way across.

'Aha, the fair Amaryllis,' said Roy. He stood up, bowed, and offered Ril a chair. The two girls giggled.

'Showroom accent again tonight,' commented Norman.

'Allow me to introduce . . .' Roy began, '. . . dear me, what

50

were these young ladies' names? I'm afraid your appearance has quite driven them out of my head.'

The girls giggled again. This was part of Roy's act.

'All right,' said Norman brusquely. 'Joke over. Ril : Eva : Sylvie. Now you know each other.'

' 'Ullo !' said Sylvie.

' 'Ow do?' said Eva.

They looked at Ril and she at them with equal curiosity. Both girls were about seventeen. Eva had her hair tinted pale pink and done up on top. It reminded Ril of candyfloss. Her face was powdered a matt white and her eyebrows heavily emphasized. She wore a good deal of green eye-shadow. Under all this Ril guessed her face to be round and homely, and her figure was sloppy. Sylvie had more about her. She had a thin, sharp, but pretty face and a thin, sharp, but pretty figure. There was a hint of shrewdness in her expression.

'Goodness, it's warm,' Ril said, by way of making conversation.

'Oh aye,' said Sylvie.

'Not 'alf,' said Eva.

'There's some in 'ere that's 'ot stuff, that's why it's warm,' said Sylvie.

'Oh, go on !' said Eva, giggling.

'If they 'ad twice as many brains they'd be a pair of 'alf-wits,' said Norman in disgust.

Ril felt some doubt about this assessment so far as Sylvie was concerned. But neither girl was offended.

'Oh, go on !' said Eva again.

'Tek no notice of our Norman,' said Sylvie. 'Mr Grizzly, that's 'im.'

Roy had listened with a weary expression.

'Amaryllis,' he said, 'would you care to tread a measure?'

'Well, if you can call it treading a measure,' said Ril. The evening had warmed up, and the floor was now packed with a jiving throng.

'One can always dance if one knows how,' said Roy. He led her into a quickstep, weaving expertly among the jivers. He and Ril were the only couple dancing conventionally on the whole floor, and they were good.

'*You* know how,' Ril said, referring to his last remark.

'One has done it before,' said Roy modestly.

'Are the two girls with you?'

'Sylvie is with me, I fear,' said Roy. 'A poor thing but mine own. Eva is merely Sylvie's friend.'

Ril was silent.

'You were thinking,' said Roy, 'that I could do better.'

'Well, since you say it yourself, I was. I wouldn't go out with a person I thought so little of.'

Roy sighed.

'Alas,' he said, 'much as one would prefer to take out a Celia Withens, one has to make do with the available material.'

Ril imagined Celia Withens among the jiving teenagers at the Rex and laughed aloud. Roy misunderstood her and was nettled.

'Why shouldn't I go out with Celia Withens?' he demanded, forgetting for a moment the showroom accent.

'I don't see why anybody shouldn't go out with anyone they like,' said Ril hastily. 'But do you think you'd have much in common?'

Roy's retort was prompt.

'Good looks and fast cars,' he said. 'And I'm making money these days. I could go to much better places than this. I want to take out a girl with style.' He reverted to the showroom accent. 'You'll admit, my dear Amaryllis, that Celia Withens has style with a capital S. I saw her shopping in town this morning. She was enchanting. A vision. If only we were acquainted . . .'

'And what would Sylvie think?' inquired Ril.

'Sylvie doesn't think.'

'Don't be so sure,' said Ril. 'Roy, I'm tired. May I sit down?'

'Certainly,' said Roy. He relinquished her hand gracefully. They returned to their table. Norman was now dancing with Eva. Sylvie and Cliff sat together, saying nothing. Sylvie was not looking pleased.

'Come on, Roy,' she said. 'Drop the lords-and-ladies stuff. Let's dance.'

Roy returned to the floor with Sylvie. They jived.

A good deal of noise was coming from the next table. Ril glanced round. There were four or five rough-looking lads there with girls to match. Jokes and insults – some of them extremely crude – were flying across the table. Ril winced.

Cliff sat watching the dancers, a wistful look in his eyes.

'Aren't you dancing tonight, Cliff?' Ril asked.

Cliff blushed.

'I can't really dance,' he said.

'Not the least little bit?'

'Well, I know some o' t'steps, like, but I allus get in a muddle. Sylvie says I've got two left feet.' He grinned bashfully.

'Never mind,' said Ril. 'As it happens, I've two right ones, so we should be all right. Come on, Cliff, let's see how we get on.'

She was not sorry to get on to the floor again. The noise from the next table had become oppressive. All the same, Cliff made heavy weather of it, walking all over her feet and keeping up a steady flow of apologies. When the dance ended she felt she had done her good deed for the day.

It was quieter now, and looking across to the next table Ril saw that the girls there were now on their own.

'Where have all the boys gone?' she asked.

'They'll be in t'Feathers, I expect,' said Norman.

'What, in a pub?'

'Oh aye. There's only soft drinks here, you see. They get a pass out. They'll be back soon.'

'Do many people do that?' asked Ril.

'Oh, quite a few,' said Eva. 'It makes a break, like. Roy an' Sylvie an' me could go, but not t'rest o' you, because you're under age. They wouldn't serve you in t'Feathers. . . . 'Ere, Roy, what about it? Goin' to buy us a drink?'

''E'll never drag 'isself away,' said Sylvie.

'Quite right, my dear,' said Roy smoothly. 'It would be most impolite. And how could I desert such charming company?'

'In case you wasn't listenin',' said Sylvie to Ril, 'that means you. 'E dun't talk to me like that, I can tell you.'

'It would be a case of pearls before –' began Roy.

'Gerr, you're the swine!' retorted Sylvie.

'Here they come now,' said Norman. The group of boys were returning to the next table. Hands in pockets, cigarettes in mouths, they swaggered back to their seats. As they went past, one of them elbowed Cliff, who drew his chair farther in. Norman's eyes narrowed, but he said nothing.

The music started. Roy and Sylvie rose to dance.

The burliest of the boys from the next table came across to Ril, raised his eyebrows, and jerked a thumb towards the dance-floor.

Ril ignored the invitation. Norman half rose from his seat.

'Well, what about a dance?' the lad demanded.

Ril didn't like refusing to dance, but this time she had no doubt.

'No, thank you,' she said. 'I'm not dancing just now.'

'Come on!' the boy said. It sounded more like a command than a request.

'You 'eard!' said Norman. 'She's not dancin' wi' you.'

The lad turned and swung a fist. Norman dodged it. Instantly there was a fight in progress. The rest of the group joined in with their leader. But it was clear that they were

54

not the only gang in the hall. Others attacked them, and were attacked in turn by still newer arrivals. A table crashed over. Girls squealed. The music and most of the dancing went on, but in the corner near the bar a free-for-all was developing. Through the corner of her eye Ril saw the management's strong-arm men approaching.

She felt a touch on her arm. It was Roy.

'You'd better get out of this!' he said rapidly. 'Come with me!'

'But what about Norman?'

'Norman can look after himself. Come on!'

In the noise and confusion it was impossible to argue. Ril allowed Roy to lead her out by an emergency exit. In the street stood the Triumph.

Ril hesitated.

'I can't just go away and leave him,' she said.

'You'll help Norman best by keeping out of trouble,' said Roy. 'And don't be alarmed, you're safe with me.' He bundled her aboard, jumped in beside her, and drove off. Five minutes later she was on the doorstep of 5, Park Terrace.

'Norman shouldn't have taken you to the Rex,' said Roy. He had dropped the showroom accent again. 'You want to keep away from places like that. Good night, Ril. . . . Are you still worrying about him?'

'Yes.'

'Well, you needn't. I'm going back there now. He'll be all right. No one's ever been murdered at the Rex. He won't get anything worse than a black eye.'

And Roy drove off.

Ril looked at her watch. It wasn't half past ten yet. She waited outside for a while, thinking that Norman might appear. But when he had not done so by a quarter to eleven she went into the flat.

'Where's your escort?' asked Robert. 'He needn't leave you on the doorstep.'

Ril said nothing. Her father looked curiously at her but made no further comment.

She was not sure how she felt. She was cross with Norman for taking her to the kind of place where a brawl could break out in public. But she liked the way he had sprung to her defence. She hoped he hadn't got a black eye.

*

Round the corner from the Rex, Norman stopped under a street-lamp to mop a cut on his cheek and inspect the damage to his best suit.

'Might 'a' bin worse,' said Cliff. 'That Jack Raynor who started it all looks a bigger mess than you, I can tell you.'

'Serve 'im right. But where's Ril?'

'I told you,' said Cliff. 'She got out.'

'Well, at least she wasn't chucked out. She wouldn't 'ave liked that. But where did she go?'

'I dunno,' said Cliff. ''Ere, gimme your 'anky. You've still got blood on your face. We can't 'ave you goin' round like this.'

'She might still be waiting for me, somewhere near the Rex. Let's go back there.'

'T'manager told you not to go near t'place again.'

'Well, 'e can't keep me off t'Queen's 'ighway, can 'e?'

'I tell you, Norm, she's all right. She'll 'ave gone 'ome by now.'

'I bet she 'asn't. Come on, Cliff, get a move on.'

' 'Ere, who's that at t'corner?'

'Blimey, it's them again.'

'Six of 'em at least. Quiet, they 'appen 'aven't seen us.'

'Oh yes, they 'ave !' said Norman grimly. 'We'd better run for it. No point in gettin' beaten up. Make for t'main road, they wouldn't dare to try anythin' there.'

Norman and Cliff ran. Jack Raynor and his gang ran after them. Footsteps echoed along the narrow side road. Somebody threw a stone, which missed Cliff by a yard. Norman stumbled, caught his foot in the kerb, and fell. Half a dozen lads closed in. But at that moment there was the roar of an exhaust and Roy's Triumph tore along the street, scattering the gang right and left. In seconds Norman and Cliff were safe in the car. More stones were thrown as it drove off, and one struck the rear bumper.

'Second rescue in twenty minutes,' said Roy. 'Norman, lad, you're keeping me busy tonight. First it's your cousin, now it's you. Where would you be without your Uncle Roy?'

'My cousin . . . You mean Ril was with you?'

'Of course she was. Somebody had to look after her, hadn't they? You were too busy.'

'Busier than you. You didn't risk gettin' hurt, did you? Anyroad, where is she now?'

'At her own home.'

'You only just ran 'er home, didn't you, Roy?'

Roy detected an undertone of anxiety in Norman's voice. On impulse he said:

'We had a little talk. She likes me, boy. She likes me.'

Norman scowled.

'She got in the car as eager as a kid grabbing a lolly,' said Roy.

Norman scowled again.

'P'raps I'll take her a longer ride one of these days,' added Roy, enjoying himself.

'Oh no, you won't.'

'That's for her to say.'

'Why, you dirty —'

Roy was delighted to find Norman so vulnerable.

'I held her hand, too,' he went on untruthfully. 'She seemed to like it.'

Norman clenched a fist.

'Look out, Roy!' said Cliff urgently.

'It's all right, I'm not goin' to bash 'im,' said Norman. ''E's not worth it. Nor is she. You can put me down 'ere, Roy Wentworth. An' you can patch up your own old crocks in future – I've finished with you.'

Roy laughed.

'Don't fret, boy, I was only kidding,' he said. 'I drove her straight home. We didn't speak a dozen words.'

Norman still scowled.

'Don't you believe me? Ask her yourself, then.'

There was a heavy silence.

'Listen, lad,' said Roy, 'if I was to tell you what I'm aiming at you'd be surprised. But it isn't baby-snatching. You needn't worry about Ril. She's only a kid. And she's a nice kid, boy – as nice as they come.'

Silence again. Then :

'She should 'a' waited for me, all the same,' said Norman.

Ril thought that Norman would probably come round the next day. She had an imaginary dialogue worked out, in which he apologized for getting her into an awkward situation and she in turn made it clear that she hadn't meant to desert him. But there was no sign of Norman all through the long, hot Sunday, or on Monday morning.

On Monday afternoon Robert Terry took his daughter into town on the tram for a shopping and sightseeing expedition. The expedition came to a premature end after twenty minutes when they arrived at a bookshop. There Robert stayed for the rest of the afternoon. Ril gave up the sightseeing as lost, but went off to complete the shopping. She returned to find her father still browsing among the shelves. She contemplated him with wry affection: a harm-less, lovable man, but lacking in drive and aggression and all the other qualities that took people to the top of their various trees. He was lucky, at nearly fifty, to have landed his new job with the extra-mural department of West Riding University. It was probably as far as he would ever get.

Ril sighed, though without much regret, for she would not have wished her father to be different. Then she stole silently up to him and whispered in his ear the one word:

'Tea.'

Robert started, looked at his watch, and apologized. He had been in the bookshop for an hour and a half.

'Take me somewhere nice,' said Ril, 'if there is anywhere nice for tea in Hallersage.'

'Certainly there's somewhere nice for tea,' said Robert. 'We'll go to Maggie's.'

Maggie's was a big, cheerful, first-floor teashop, with pot-ted palms, and a score of waitresses bustling round, and the babble of a hundred conversations, and a trio sawing away hopefully at Strauss waltzes amid the uproar. Ril ate toast and drank tea, and pondered – without any great sense of urgency – her next move in the matter of the old Common.

The customers at Maggie's were mostly comfortable middle-aged ladies. But there was an exception: at a table near the Terrys' were two young men and a girl, and under cover of the general noise they were carrying on a lively argument. Ril studied them with interest. The girl was in her early twenties. She was dark, decisive, and crisply pretty, and she wore a dazzling white blouse like an advertisement for soap-flakes. The first young man was small, dark, and decisive too, and he fascinated Ril by the way he threw him-self into the argument – gesturing, thumping the table, and sometimes positively bouncing up and down with excite-ment. The second young man had his back to Ril. He was large and comparatively restrained. Only when he turned sideways for a moment did Ril realize that she had met him before.

'Why, it's James Willoughby!' she said. 'You know, the young man who lives in the flat above ours.'

'I know,' said Robert. 'The one who likes Hallersage. He hasn't a lot to say at the moment, has he?'

'His friends make up for him,' said Ril.

And indeed the sparks were flying between the other two. They were interrupting each other and capping each other's remarks, and once the girl, laughing, tried to cuff the young man over the ear.

Just then came one of those curious moments when every conversation in earshot halts at the same time and the silence can be heard a mile away. The only person unaware of it was the small young man, and he went straight on, with his voice rising as he reached the peak of his argument, and his words tumbling over one another.

'Why,' he said, 'why, it's like – it's like – it's like lipstick on a rhinoceros!'

The last few words fell plumb into the silence and were heard all over Maggie's café. Everyone stared. The girl and the young man grinned, not caring. At that moment James Willoughby looked round, recognized the Terrys, and went over to their table.

'Good afternoon,' he said. 'It's nice to see you.' And then, 'If you've finished your tea, perhaps you'd care to join us?'

He introduced his companions. The small young man was Kenneth Ryder, and he was an architect. The girl was Barbara Carr, and she taught at the local art school. She and Kenneth were engaged.

'And now,' said Ril, 'tell us who's the rhinoceros.'

'The rhinoceros,' said Kenneth, 'is Hallersage High Street.'

Ril blinked.

'You see,' explained Barbara, 'Kenneth has Plans. Glor-

60

ious plans. He thinks the centre of Hallersage should be Swept Away.' She illustrated the sweeping away with a gesture of her arm.

'Mind those teacups,' said James.

'And come to the point, girl, can't you?' said Kenneth. 'What I was just saying was that instead of pulling down all those horrid gloomy Victorian buildings they just slap modern shop-fronts across them. And it looks awful. That's what I meant by lipstick on a rhinoceros. Now what they ought to do is this. . . .'

He grabbed a paper napkin and drew rapidly on it in pencil, at the same time volubly outlining his views on town centres in general and Hallersage town centre in particular. Ril had never realized before how a person's profession could be a passion. Robert was impressed, and put in several questions.

After a minute or two James interrupted.

'Kenneth,' he said, 'I'd like these people to see our model. Why don't you run us all up to the flat? That is, if Mr Terry's finished his business in town.'

Robert accepted the offer. Bills were paid. Everyone trooped down to the street and got into Kenneth's Morris Minor. Kenneth let in the clutch with alarming suddenness, and the car leaped forward. After fifty yards it came to traffic-lights and stopped just as suddenly.

'Splendid brakes,' said Kenneth with satisfaction.

The lights changed and the car shot forward again. Kenneth's driving was like his speech – impetuous and rapid. Luckily his reactions were quick. In Park Terrace the Morris stopped with a final jolt and its occupants went up the stairs, past the Terrys' flat, and into James's. And there the room which should have been the sitting-room was almost filled with a scale model of a town centre.

At first Ril could not tell what town it was. The buildings, beautifully modelled, were all modern. Some were tall

61

and dramatic, some were long and low and arcaded. All were light and airy with acres of glass. There were paved squares and gardens and a bandstand, and the toy traffic was all routed round a wide circular road with bridges over it for pedestrians.

'Where is it meant to be . . . ?' Ril began, and then she noticed in the middle a familiar turreted stone building. It was Hallersage Town Hall, and next to it were the Law Courts. And now that she looked more closely the old covered market and a handful more of the existing buildings were there as well. But all that was dreariest in Hallersage had been thrown out, to be replaced by bright new buildings and open spaces.

'Why, it's a new Hallersage!' Ril exclaimed; and then, awestruck, she asked, 'Are you going to build that?'

'Of course we are!' said Kenneth.

'I wish we could!' said James.

'It's the perfect city,' said Kenneth. 'And I ought to know. I designed it.'

'Modesty,' said Barbara, 'is not Kenneth's besetting sin.'

'Well, I think it's lovely,' said Ril.

'Too much glass,' said Barbara.

'It's the Hallersage of tomorrow!' Kenneth declared. 'When we've built this we'll really be on the map. Hallersage will be the town-planners' Mecca.'

'Too much glass,' said Barbara again. 'Not practical.'

'She doesn't know what she's talking about,' said Kenneth.

'What will it all cost?' inquired Robert mildly.

'A good question, sir. A good question,' Kenneth admitted. 'Well, we could make a useful start with five or six million pounds.'

'And how much have you got?'

'Fifteen pounds, four and tuppence,' said Kenneth ruefully.

'It's a dream, I'm afraid,' said James, 'though we hope it

may give rise to something. You remember I mentioned the New Hallersage Society to you? Well, this is what it's for. A few of us formed it last year to promote this scheme, or something like it.'

'And what are you going to do?' asked Robert.

'We were hoping to exhibit the model in the City Art Gallery, but they won't let us. And we circularized the councillors, only none of them replied. Still, we mean to get moving when autumn comes. We shall book a hall and exhibit it ourselves and see what support we get.'

'And do you think that will bring in the millions?'

'Frankly,' said James, 'I don't.' He sighed.

'Doesn't it worry you,' asked Robert seriously, 'to spend a lot of energy on a project that may never come to anything?'

'You mean, aren't we wasting our time?' said James. 'I don't think so. I admit there are all sorts of difficulties. But, you see, this is an idea to work in people's minds. So long as we can keep the vision alive – that one day we're going to have a new Hallersage – then we're doing some good. It's a matter of the climate of opinion.'

'Weather forecast: continuing mainly damp,' said Barbara.

'You ought to get Sam Thwaite interested,' suggested Ril.

'Sam Thwaite?' said Kenneth. 'Not a hope. He thinks I'm mad.'

'Can't blame him for that,' said Barbara.

'Just wait till we're married, girl. I shall beat you, see if I don't!'

James wasn't joining in the insults. He went on slowly from where he had left off.

'One day,' he said, 'the climate of opinion will change. And we're going to do our bit in changing it. And the day will come when a plan – perhaps like this, perhaps quite different – will really be put into effect. And that will justify everything.'

He was so earnest that Ril found him almost funny – except that it warmed her heart to see somebody believing in something to that extent. Suddenly his enthusiasm revived her determination to see if she could do something about Old Hallersage Common – and do it quickly. In comparison with the task that Kenneth and James had set themselves, hers seemed almost easy.

Later, when she and Robert had gone down to their own flat and she was cooking the supper, she pondered the new Hallersage at length. True, the present Hallersage was an ugly, dirty, congested place. But she could imagine two comments on Kenneth's perfect city all too easily. In the mind's ear she could hear Sam Thwaite saying, 'I never saw owt so daft in my life.' And she could guess what Norman would say, too. 'I'm not interested in all this airy-fairy stuff. There's nowt wrong with 'Allersage as it is.'

The Northern character was awkward, she decided; very awkward.

Besides, they might well be right.

'Here you are, Ril,' she said to herself, 'here you are at this moment making a cheese soufflé. Time you learned to cook tripe.' She shuddered at the thought.

Still, she consoled herself, there couldn't be two ways of thinking about the old Common. Whatever they felt about a new city, everyone would be glad if that could be recovered.

She remembered Sam Thwaite's advice to 'talk to t'owd lady', and Florrie's remarks on the evening of her arrival in Hallersage.

It was high time she saw Great-Aunt Martha.

*

'Why, come in, Ril love!' cried Florrie warmly. 'We was hopin' you'd come an' see us soon. 'Ow are you? 'Ow's your dad?'

'I'm fine and he's fine,' said Ril, 'and he's gone to Leeds today on business.'

'Are y'on your own, then? Well, you must stay for your tea.'

'Oh no, please don't bother. . . .'

'Nonsense. Of course you must. We've got plenty. I'll oppen a tin o' salmon. It's right good salmon. T'best. I 'ad it for last Christmas, but you get that much to eat at Christmas it outfaces you. Or I could slip out an' get some 'am an' tongue. Would you like that?'

'I'll have a bit of whatever you were going to have,' said Ril. 'I don't really eat much tea as a rule.'

Florrie looked anxious.

'I 'ope you're eatin' enough,' she said. 'A young lass like you lookin' after t'house, and your dad so absent-minded 'e wouldn't know if 'e'd 'ad 'is dinner or not. I 'ope you're not livin' on bread-an'-butter an' cups o' tea.'

'We eat very well,' said Ril.

'Tell me what you 'ad last night,' demanded Florrie.

'I made a cheese soufflé.'

'There you are!' cried Florrie triumphantly. 'Nowt but a bit o' foreign nonsense. What you need is some good roast beef an' Yorkshire puddin'. That'd put t'roses in your cheeks.' She looked Ril up and down. 'Though I must say you're gettin' to be a bonny lass. I know our Norman thinks so, anyroad.'

'Does he?' Ril asked with interest.

'Oh aye. 'E thinks a lot of you, does our Norman.'

'But he argues with me all the time.'

'Oh well, that's 'is way,' explained Florrie. 'Independent, like. 'E thinks you're cleverer than what 'e is, but 'e won't let you get t'better of 'im.'

'I don't think I'm cleverer,' said Ril thoughtfully. 'Just different.'

'Did you 'ave a nice time on Sat'day?' asked Florrie.

'Yes, very nice, thank you,' Ril answered cautiously. 'Did Norman tell you about it?'

''E didn't tell me much. 'E never does. I 'ad a job to get out of 'im 'ow 'e fell in t'street an' cut 'is cheek. I can't think 'ow 'e managed to do it. Eh, lads are clumsy. And 'e still 'asn't told me where 'e took you.' She looked at Ril inquiringly.

'We went to the Rex,' said Ril with some reluctance.

Florrie tut-tutted.

'Well, 'e oughter 'a' took you somewhere better than that. They're a rough lot that go to t'Rex. Eh, I don't know what you'll think of us.'

'Now just you stop worrying,' said Ril. 'I had a lovely time. Can I help you make the tea?'

She was trying to think of a way of turning the conversation to Great-Aunt Martha. But Florrie had still not finished with the topic of Saturday evening. She went to the foot of the stairs.

'Norman!' she called. 'Norma-a-an!'

Ril hadn't realized that Norman was in the house.

''E's in 'is den,' Florrie explained. 'In t'attic. Eh, you should see t'junk 'e 'as up there. Allus mekkin' summat or mendin' summat.'

None too promptly, Norman appeared. He looked sullen on seeing Ril.

''Ullo,' he said. 'Well, what is it, Mum?'

'Now, Norman lad,' said Florrie, 'what d'you mean by takin' Ril to t'Rex? There's better places than that in 'Allersage, isn't there?'

Norman frowned. 'I've taken 'er now,' he said. 'It's 'istory.'

'I was just saying what a nice time we had,' said Ril hastily.

'Oh aye? Well, I'm glad you enjoyed y'self.'

''Oo was you with?' demanded Florrie.

66

'Roy Wentworth,' said Norman. 'And Eva Jones and Cliff Longbottom and Sylvie Woodward.'

Florrie sniffed.

'A right lot o' good-for-nothin's to introduce your cousin to,' she said in disgust. 'All except Cliff. Cliff'd be a nice lad if 'e 'ad t'chance.'

'Ril needn't 'ave come if she 'adn't wanted,' said Norman. 'I don't know what you're fussin' about. She can take us as she finds us. We're not like 'er stuck-up Southern friends, so what's t'use o' pretendin'?'

'Well, that's not t'way you was talkin' about Ril last week,' said Florrie in surprise.

Norman reddened.

'Well, it's t'way I'm talkin' now,' he said sullenly.

'You 'aven't fell out, 'ave you?' asked Florrie anxiously.

'We 'aven't fell *in*, that I know of.'

'Now look 'ere, Norman Clough,' said Florrie, 'it's about time you remembered your manners.'

'Manners!' echoed Norman bitterly. 'It's a question of manners, is it? Everything on t'surface. Let's all be nice to each other. . . . Gerr! There's more important things than manners, if you ask me.'

'That'll do!' said Florrie sharply. 'Sit down an' get on wi' your tea!'

Norman looked thunderous but sat down. Florrie asked some questions about Robert's work and about household arrangements, and drifted gradually into neighbourhood gossip, of which she had an endless supply. Norman said not a word, and as soon as he had finished pushed his plate away and disappeared upstairs.

'Well,' sighed Florrie, 'summat's upset t'lad. I don't know what it is.'

Ril decided she must sort things out with Norman later. But she had not forgotten the main aim of her visit.

'Can I see the old lady?' she asked.

Florrie stared.

'Aunt Martha?' she said. 'What d'you want to see Aunt Martha for?'

'I just thought I'd like to meet her.'

'But she's old, Ril love, she's old. She'll be a hundred in just over a year, if she lives that long. You're just beginnin' your life, pet – you don't want to see folks that's endin' it.'

'Don't you think *she* might like to see *me*?'

'Nay, love, she dun't know owt about you. We don't bother 'er wi' things these days. Besides, she's wanderin' in 'er mind a bit. She was all right until t'start o' this year – a wonderful old lady, folks used to say. But she's not so well now – not well at all.'

Florrie sighed.

'What's wrong with her?' Ril asked.

'Well, I don't know that there's anything exactly wrong with 'er, except old age. She keeps sayin' she's tired, like. And so would I be if I was as old as that. It'll be a mercy when she's passed on.'

'Where is she now?'

'She's still in 'er own 'ouse, at t'back o' t'block 'ere. It's t'same 'ouse as she were born in, and she wouldn't stand to be moved now. These last few weeks she's 'ad a nurse with 'er. Before that I used to do a bit o' cookin' an' cleanin' for 'er, an' she managed on 'er own. She was right proud, you know.'

'Would it upset her if I were to see her?'

'I don't suppose so,' said Florrie. 'We thought it was you that might be upset. Though she's quite calm an' peaceful, I must say.'

A shrewd look came into Florrie's eye.

'But you're wantin' summat, aren't you, Ril Terry? I'll lay a pound it's to do wi' t'old Common.'

'Well, yes,' Ril admitted. 'Daddy told me how Caradoc

68

Clough said it would come back to the people of Hallersage one day. And only last week I heard that some people say the Common could be got back if everyone knew their rights.'

'They think Aunt Martha knows summat about it, eh?'

'Well, that's what I gathered.'

'Aye,' said Florrie grimly. 'Well, Aunt Martha does know summat about it. Summat that owd Caradoc told 'er 'isself. But I won't 'ave anyone botherin' 'er with it now, an' that's flat.'

'I wouldn't dream of bothering an old lady of that age,' said Ril. 'But I admit I'm curious. I'd like to find out all I can.'

'Well, you know what Fred thinks about it,' said Florrie. 'An' all t'Cloughs is t'same. They'd rather it was dead an' buried. Many a time I 'eard Fred's dad stop folks talkin' about it. "There's no good'll come of interferin' wi' t'past," 'e used to say. "What's done is done." I can 'ear 'im sayin' it now. An' as for Norman, 'e calls it 'istory, an' 'e reckons nowt to 'istory. "'Istory is bunk," 'e says.'

'Henry Ford said that,' Ril told her. 'But I don't believe it. Long live the past, say I.'

'Long live t'past,' echoed Florrie thoughtfully. 'Ril love, I don't know that I ought to, but I'm goin' to tell you t'rest o' what I know about t'Cloughs and t'owd Common. After all, you're a Clough yourself, an' you've as much right to know as anyone. But don't you be gettin' any fancy ideas. Now, put that dishcloth away, and there'll just be time to tell you before I start gettin' Fred's supper ready.'

'Well, now,' said Florrie comfortably as she sat back with a
fresh cup of tea in her hand, 'you know 'ow old Caradoc
Clough led them there rebels, and 'ow they was put down by
t'troops. An' Caradoc was 'ad up for it an' transported. That
means they sent 'im to Australia.

''E was away for seven year, an' then 'e come back to
'Allersage – to Old 'Allersage, that is, because t'new town
was 'ardly started in them days – and 'e lived t'rest of 'is
life in a 'ouse just at t'other side o' t'square from 'ere. 'E lived
to be ower eighty, and Aunt Martha remembers 'im quite
well, an' a queer crusty old chap 'e was in 'is old age, from
what she says. 'E'd learned t'trade of a joiner, and 'e worked
a good deal on t'buildin' o' t'new town – mills an' factories
an' 'ouses an' all t'lot – but when Aunt Martha knew 'im
'e'd given up steady work, though 'e'd still do an odd job if
'e felt like it.

'Now Sir George Withens, who'd sent 'im down, was
another crusty old chap, in fact 'im an' Caradoc was quite a
pair, because they both liked their own way an' they both
thought they was allus right. Well, one day, accordin' to
Aunt Martha, Sir George an' Caradoc meet, an' Sir George
gives Caradoc a piece of 'is mind, an' Caradoc gives 'im a
piece back, which in them days was summat that t'workin'
folk never did to their betters. And Sir George was right took
aback, but after a bit 'e laughs.'

'Yes, I can imagine it,' said Ril. She twirled imaginary
moustaches and spoke in a tone she thought suitable for an
English squire of the early nineteenth century: 'Damme if
the fella hasn't got a point, what? Clough, you're an impu-

dent rogue but I'll buy you a pint of ale in the Feathers, damme if I don't.'

'Well, I don't suppose it was like that,' said Florrie doubtfully. 'From what I 'ear, old Sir George was just a 'ard-'eaded Yorkshireman like t'rest of 'em, except that 'e 'appened to be t'gaffer. Anyroad, 'im an' Caradoc got quite pally, like, and if Sir George 'adn't owt else to do 'e sometimes used to send t'carriage to take Caradoc up to Withishall for a talk an' a sup and 'appen a game of dominoes or summat.

'From time to time they used to argue, of course, about t'owd Common, but they never got nowhere. Sir George was 'ard, like all t'Withenses, an' wasn't likely to give owt away. But after 'is son was killed in t'Indian Mutiny 'e changed. 'E lost interest in 'is farmin' experiments, and 'e began to get it into 'is 'ead that Caradoc 'ad been right after all, an' that losin' 'is son was a judgement on 'im. And one day 'e told Caradoc 'e'd made an addition to 'is will, leavin' t'Common back again to t'people of 'Allersage.

'A year or two later 'e died – 'e was turned eighty – and 'is will was read, but there was nowt in it about t'Common, and it passed with all t'rest to Sir George's grandson, Sir William, and 'e was t'meanest old stick that ever lived at Withishall, an' that's sayin' summat. Caradoc never did owt about what Sir George 'ad told 'im, because 'e was seventy 'isself, and 'e'd become a bit of a ... You know, one 'oo takes what people say with a pinch o' salt.'

'A cynic?' suggested Ril.

'That's right, a cynic. 'E thought that what Sir George 'ad said about leavin' t'Common back to t'town was just words, and that Sir George 'ad never meant to do it. But shortly before Caradoc died young Lady Withens – that was Sir William's wife – come down from t'hall in 'er carriage to see 'im. She was right proper distressed, from what Aunt Martha told me, and she told Caradoc that Sir George 'ad left a message for 'im, but that 'er 'usband 'ad tore it up. And what it was about was this – that Sir George 'ad wrote a piece on to 'is will about t'Common, after all, but 'e 'adn't done it through t'lawyers because 'e thought there'd be trouble about it if 'e did. And although young Sir William 'ad destroyed t'note, she knew what was in it. It was instructions to find this extra bit o' will. And so t'young madam passed t'message on to Caradoc by word o' mouth. And Caradoc passed it on to Aunt Martha.'

'And what was it?' demanded Ril.

'Ah, well, that I can't tell you,' said Florrie. 'Aunt Martha says she knows. But all she's ever told us was a jumble o' words that didn't mean owt. She must 'a' got it wrong. Or 'appen she's forgot it durin' all these years.'

Florrie put down her teacup.

'I'll 'ave to think about lettin' you see 'er. I'm not sayin' you can and I'm not sayin' you can't. And now I must go an' start makin' Fred's supper. 'E'll be back from work any minute now.'

*

Though Ril had listened with interest to Florrie's tale, she had been worrying all the time in a corner of her mind about Norman's resentment. When Florrie disappeared into the kitchen she ran lightly up the stairs and tapped on the attic door.

Norman was sprawling on the floor with the parts of a two-stroke engine scattered round him. He looked up as she entered, and frowned.

'Norman, thank you for sticking up for me the other night.'

'That was nowt,' said Norman shortly. 'I'd 'ave done it for anyone.'

'Well, I'm glad you did it for me.'

Norman jabbed aimlessly at a piece of metal with a screwdriver, but said nothing.

'Are you cross with me?' Ril asked.

Silence.

'I'm sorry if I seemed to go off and leave you in the lurch. I didn't know what to do. I could hardly have joined in the fight, could I?'

'I don't blame you for gettin' out o' t'way o' t'scrap,' said Norman. 'It does no good to 'ave girls around, and they might get 'urt. But you could 'a' waited for me, couldn't you, instead o' goin' off wi' a feller like that?'

Ril stared.

'You mean Roy? He ran me home, that's all.'

'Aye, I know 'e ran you 'ome. 'E conducted the fair Amaryllis to 'er place of residence.' Bitterness flooded into Norman's voice. 'Well, if you want to know, I reckon nowt to a lass that goes out wi' one lad an' comes back wi' another. There's summat we value 'ere in t'North, though 'appen you've never 'eard of it where you come from. It's loyalty.'

Ril, feeling herself partly in the wrong, had been willing to accept a reproof. But this last attack was not to be borne. She flared up.

'What a hateful thing to say!' she cried. 'What sort of person do you think I am? I suppose this is your Northern bluntness. You seem to think it's a virtue to be rude to people. Stupid, oafish vanity I call it.' She was warming up now. 'Well, if you want to know what I think about the North, I think it's an ugly, bleak, dirty place, full of pig-headed, narrow-minded people, and I wish I'd never set foot in it!'

She marched out, slamming the door.

Halfway down the stairs she began to feel less cross. Going out of the front door she regretted her outburst. By the time she reached the street corner she was ashamed of herself.

She turned, let herself into Florrie's house again, and crept upstairs. She tapped on the attic door and pushed it open. Norman had sunk to the floor again but wasn't getting on with his work. He was gazing vacantly into the middle distance.

'Norman!'

''Lo, Ril!'

'Norman, I'm sorry.'

'All right, forget it.'

'It was partly your own fault, you know. After all, you took me to that place.'

'Aye,' said Norman. 'Aye, that's true.' He was subdued now.

'And I'm not a disloyal person. That wasn't fair.'

'I suppose not.'

'Your mother told me something about you the day I arrived here,' said Ril; and added softly and clearly: 'Norman Caradoc Clough.'

Norman reddened.

'What did she 'ave to tell you that for?' he demanded crossly.

'Well, you can't keep your name a secret,' Ril pointed out.

'Nobody knows at school, or among t'lads,' said Norman, 'and I'll thank you not to tell 'em. It sounds that daft! Caradoc!'

'I'd have thought it was something to be proud of,' said Ril. 'And you're not short of pride, are you, Norman C. Clough?'

'I don't claim no credit for what my great-grandpa did. I'll stand on my own feet, thank you.'

'But, Norman,' Ril went on, 'doesn't it stir your blood to think of this ancestor of yours? A man on the point of being transported, and he dares to speak as he did. And he claimed that the people would get the Common back, but they haven't got it yet. Doesn't that make you want to go out and do something about it?'

Her eyes were eager. Norman felt a sudden conviction that he had misjudged her.

'Ril,' he said. 'You're all right. I must be daft. You're all right.'

'Of course I'm all right. None righter. Are we friends?'

'Aye,' said Norman. 'We are that.' Then, with an effort: 'I'm sorry.'

Ril decided to appeal to him.

'Norman, even if it does seem a bit silly to you will you help me to find out what I can about the Caradoc thing, just as a matter of interest?'

'I'll 'elp you,' said Norman warily, 'if you know what you're goin' to do.'

'I don't really,' Ril admitted. 'But there's one thing I'd like to do as soon as I can, and that's to see inside the Withens wall. Have you ever been in there?'

'Aye, I've been in there,' said Norman. 'It's never open to t'public, you know. But I've been in with another lad, swimmin' in t'river. I know where you can get over t'wall. We was there early in t'mornin'. It was fun.'

'If you've done it once you can do it again, can't you?' asked Ril.

'Are you a swimmer, Ril?'

'I'm a very good one.'

'Well, this is t' swimmin' season, isn't it? I'll call for you at 'alf past six on Sat'day mornin'. Put on your costume under your clothes. We'll go for a swim in t'Withishall grounds. Nobody'll catch us at that time.'

'It's a date,' said Ril.

'But don't tell anyone,' said Norman, 'neither before nor afterwards.'

*

Ril went downstairs once more. Florrie was greeting her husband in the little dark hall.

'You'll find your supper in t'oven,' she told him. 'I've made you a nice meat-an'-tatie pie. An' now I'm just slippin' across to Aunt Martha's. I'll be back in a couple o' ticks.'

Ril caught her eye. She didn't dare to ask if she could go as well. But Florrie had been thinking about the subject in the last few minutes.

'You can come wi' me if you like, Ril love,' she said.

'You're sure it won't upset her?'

'Not if you keep quiet. She probably won't even notice you. But no questions, mind!'

They set out through the backyard, across an alleyway, and in through the back door of another little stone house. Florrie trod with elaborate care. Ril followed. The house was silent: clean, tidy, but deserted-looking.

They went upstairs. Florrie tapped almost soundlessly on the first door. A nurse opened it and motioned them in.

'She's sleeping,' whispered the nurse. 'I'll leave you with her.'

'She's sleepin',' repeated Florrie unnecessarily to Ril.

They tiptoed one to each side of the bed. On the pillow lay a little thin grey head. The skin was frail but clear, the breathing faint but regular. The hump in the bed-clothes was so small it might have been made by a child.

They watched in silence for a minute. Then Aunt Martha's eyes fluttered open. They were blue, Ril noticed. Two or three times they opened and closed; then the old lady turned over to rest the other cheek on the pillow. It looked as though she was settling down again. A last flicker of the eyelids, a little sleepy sigh.

Then she saw Ril.

A startled look dawned on the old face. Aunt Martha began to struggle upright, clutching the bedclothes.

Florrie eased her into a sitting position and propped her up with pillows.

Aunt Martha's lips moved – noiselessly at first. Then a thin little voice emerged.

'Eh, thou gave me a fright,' she said faintly. 'I'd 'a' sworn

76

it was my sister Margaret, dead these eighty year. 'Oo is she, Florrie?'

Florrie went to the bed-head and spoke loudly in the old lady's ear.

'She's your great-niece. Bob Terry's lass.'

'Oh aye,' said Aunt Martha. 'Oh aye.' She looked Ril up and down with interest. 'She's t'spitten image o' Margaret, she is that. I thowt I must 'a' died an' met 'er in 'eaven. Come closer, love.'

Ril leaned over the bedside and kissed the old lady's cheek. Aunt Martha was still not quite convinced.

'Thou'rt flesh an' blood, aren't thou, lass, not an angel?'

'I'm flesh and blood,' said Ril firmly. She took the thin little hand in her own.

'Aye well, it's all for t'best. It wouldn't do in 'eaven for 'er to be as young as you an' me to be as old as me, would it, seein' we was sisters? But, eh, it's like a miracle lookin' at you. I've thowt of 'er every day these eighty year, an' now it's as if she'd come back. She wa' nobbut your age when she died. Seventeen.'

'I'm only fifteen,' said Ril.

'They grow up quick these days,' said Florrie.

'I can remember walkin' ower t'fields with 'er, lower down t'valley,' said Aunt Martha, 'when there wasn't a 'ouse to be seen. It was all country then, an' just look at it now. An' another thing I can remember . . .'

The old lady's eyes had brightened, and there was a faint colour in her cheeks.

'Now don't get excited, Auntie,' admonished Florrie.

'Don't fuss, Florrie!' said Aunt Martha sharply. 'I'm better nor I've been for months. It's a right tonic for me, seein' t'lass. She's bonny, i'n't she? Margaret were allus t'bonny 'un. I'll lay she's clever an' all. Margaret wa' clever, she was that. . . .'

A thought occurred to the old lady.

'I wonder if she'd make owt o' yon message my grandpa gave me. Margaret would 'a' known what it meant if she'd still been alive.'

Florrie's eye met Ril's across the bed, but she said nothing.

''Ave you told 'er it, Florrie?'

'Nay, I can't remember it myself, exactly,' said Florrie. 'Fred never likes to talk about it, you know.'

'Fred!' said the old lady scornfully. 'I never reckoned owt to Fred. 'E'd be scared to put two an' two together in case it came to five. Let t'lass 'ear it, Florrie. My grandpa thowt it were important. I'd 'a' liked Margaret to 'ave 'eard it, and it feels as if I was givin' it 'er now. Come 'ere love, an' kiss me again. What's thy name?'

Ril decided not to trouble her with the full version.

'I'm Ril,' she said.

'Eh, t'names they give 'em these days! Ril! Well, to me thou seems like Margaret. Now, what was I sayin'? I was goin' to tell thee summat.'

Ril was silent.

'Oh aye, I was goin' to give thee my grandpa's message. I 'ad it in my mind as clear as day a minute ago.'

Aunt Martha's face clouded. She was groping now. Her eye met Ril's blankly – so blankly that Ril thought she had lost the thread and would never give the message after all.

Then the smile came back to Aunt Martha's lips.

'I've got it now,' she announced. 'Listen carefully, love, listen carefully.'

Never was advice less needed. Ril leaned forward.

'This is it, love.' Aunt Martha spoke slowly; she was hesitant and deliberate at the same time, like a child repeating a lesson learned by heart. '"It's not behind the night thoughts." Listen again, Margaret – nay, not Margaret – anyroad, listen again, love, because I'm tellin' thee my grandpa's message. 'E said, "It's not behind the *night thoughts*."'

Ril stared.

78

'Is – is that all of it?' she asked.

Aunt Martha looked worried.

'Aye, that's it,' she said. 'That's what 'e said, exactly. Many's t'time I've said it ower to myself. My grandpa 'isself didn't know what it meant. 'E only got it a week or two before 'e died, an' it worried 'im. 'E kept sayin' Margaret'd 'a' made summat of it, if she'd been alive. She 'ad more schoolin' than t'rest of us, you know, an' she was quick on t'uptake.'

She sighed.

'Eh, love, is t'message no good to thee?'

Hastily Ril smiled.

'Of course it is,' she said. 'I'm glad you told me. I'm ever so interested.'

'Aye, that's t'truth,' said Florrie. 'She was all agog to 'ear it. She'll soon work it out, I reckon.'

Aunt Martha smiled and went on smiling, but said no more. After a minute or two her eyes closed. She had slipped back into sleep with the ease of the very old.

'Well!' declared Florrie, when the nurse had returned and she and Ril had left the sickroom. 'Well, I never did! She gave you t'message right away, an' without askin', too.'

'I hope she'll be all right,' said Ril. 'I was a bit worried.'

'Oh, she's champion,' said Florrie. 'It's like she said, it'll 'ave done 'er good to see you. Now, love, what's it all about? Did t'message mean owt to you?'

Ril pulled a face.

'Not a thing,' she said. 'Not a blessed thing.'

Norman tapped at the door. Ril was waiting for him. It was half past six on Saturday morning, and he was exactly on time.

They went out into Park Terrace. The sky was blue and cloudless, the sun shining already. It was early in August. The tiny park was ablaze with dahlias. Later in the day it would be hot again: too hot. But now it was a perfect summer morning.

Ril felt happiness bubbling up inside her. For a split second Belhampton came into her mind, but she threw it out again. To be alive – alive to your very finger-tips – on so fine a summer day: that was enough for the moment.

She threw her rolled towel in the air, ran forward, and caught it. She threw it again, but Norman darted in and intercepted.

'Catch!' he called, and threw her a Rugby pass.

Ril took the pass and called, 'Catch!' in turn, but threw the towel neatly into his face. She had recovered it and was away by the time he regained his balance.

Norman chased her. Ril ran her fastest but was caught after fifty yards. Norman grabbed her round the waist.

'Say you're sorry!'

'I'm not sorry!'

He pretended to twist her arm. They were both laughing.

'Are you sorry now?'

'No, I'm not!'

Ril ducked and wriggled, and was away again. Norman chased her once more. They were across Old Hallersage market-place before he could get near her.

The road now ran uphill to the Withens wall. Ril collapsed breathless.

'I'm sorry!' she cried, laughing. 'Sorry! Sorry! Oh, let me go!'

There was a mock scuffle before Norman released her. They walked on amicably, side by side, not jarring on each other any more.

Ril looked up at the Withens wall. It was meant to keep people out, there was no doubt about that. It was twelve feet high, of local stone, mortared and in good repair. Along the top of it, embedded in concrete, ran a row of spikes.

'You'd think it was meant to withstand a siege,' she said.

'Aye,' said Norman.

'Seems to illustrate the Withens mentality, from what I've heard of it,' Ril went on. 'Their motto's *Quod teneo tenebo*. That's Latin for "You'll get no change out of me".'

'Aye,' said Norman.

'You never know,' mused Ril. 'Perhaps they really did think they might be besieged one day. Perhaps they were afraid there'd be a people's revolt on a bigger scale than Caradoc's.'

'Mebbe,' said Norman.

'You're not really interested, are you?'

'Not much.'

Ril sighed.

'What *are* you interested in, Norman?'

'Makin' things an' doin' things.'

'But not in ideas?'

'Not unless they're useful. Not unless there's summat to see at the end o' them. This 'istory stuff isn't practical.'

'I'm going to make it practical!' declared Ril.

'Well, you can start bein' practical now. This is where we get over t'wall.'

They had reached a place where a tree branch extended over the wall towards them, just above the spikes.

'I'll give you a lift up,' said Norman.

Ril climbed on to his shoulders and locked her hands round the branch. Under her weight it bent towards the ground, and Norman held the end.

'All right, off you go,' he said. Ril edged her way along the branch and got safely over the spikes. At the Withens side the tree was easy to climb. She went down a little way and jumped to the ground. Norman followed.

'That was neat,' he said approvingly.

They were in a well-wooded corner of the grounds. Norman led the way from the wall. Soon they crossed a ride, from which the hall could be glimpsed: a stone Georgian building with various outcrops and additions. A minute or two later they came to the river. Here it was wide and shallow, rippling over stones, with open grassland at the other side. But a little way down it formed a pool, shaded and well hidden.

'What a lovely spot!' said Ril. 'I'd like to come here on a hot afternoon.'

'I wouldn't if I was you,' said Norman. 'There's two keepers, and they're as keen as mustard. Dogs, too.'

He didn't look entirely happy.

'I don't suppose they'll be about at this time,' he went on, 'but I reckon we'd better not stay too long. Just a quick swim, to say we've been, like. And then off out, quick.'

They were soon in the water. It was deep enough for swimming, though not for diving. But it was cold. At first Ril could hardly breathe. She swam two or three breadths of the pool, which was possibly twenty feet wide. Norman splashed water at her and she splashed him back. He tried to duck her, but there was not enough depth. They were both shivering.

'You're not c-c-cold, are you?' said Norman.

'Warm as toast!' declared Ril untruthfully.

'I'll race you to the other bank and back. Then let's come out.'

Ril struck out in a fast crawl for the other bank. Norman reached it a second behind her. They turned. And then they saw they were not alone. Between the two neat piles of their clothes sat a young woman.

She watched them with mild interest. She puffed at a cigarette. She looked entirely at ease. And she had a right to be at ease, for she was on her own land.

It was Celia Withens.

Teeth chattering with cold, Norman and Ril waded back across the pool. It would have seemed impertinent to swim. They stood in front of Miss Withens, side by side.

Ril had never in her life felt at such a disadvantage. Celia's elbow rested on Norman's clothes, and her book lay on top of Ril's. Coolly she looked them up and down.

'Miss Amaryllis Terry, I believe,' she said thoughtfully.

'Y-y-yes,' said Ril. Cold and nervousness made her stammer.

'Miss Terry has just come here from the South,' said Celia, as if introducing her to some imaginary third party. 'She went to a progressive school, is intrigued by sports cars, and has little sense of private property. That is all I know about her at the moment. And her friend is . . . ?'

'Norman Clough,' said Norman.

'Also of Hallersage Grammar School?'

Norman and Ril shot nervous glances at each other and nodded.

Suddenly Celia laughed.

'God, you look funny,' she said. 'Here, you'll catch your deaths. Go and get your clothes on. But don't run away. I want to talk to you.'

Ril went one way into the trees, Norman the other. They reappeared, dressed, at the same moment. Ril still felt chilly but was more self-possessed.

'Well, here we all are,' said Celia. 'A dawn encounter, you might call it. Ten past seven, to be precise. Why so early?'

'We came early because we didn't think we'd be caught at this time,' said Norman honestly.

With returning warmth Ril began to feel more like herself.

'We could ask you the same,' she said daringly.

Celia turned the slow, cool look at her.

'I don't sleep well,' she said.

She took out her cigarette case and offered it to each of them. Ril refused. So, after a moment's hesitation, did Norman. Celia lit another cigarette, inhaled, and blew out the smoke reflectively.

'Do people often come in here?' she inquired.

'Not that I know of,' said Norman. 'T'keepers are too keen.'

'Good,' said Celia. 'I'm glad to hear it. They're told to be keen. . . . You look surprised, Amaryllis.'

'Well, yes, I am,' said Ril. 'It seems funny to have somebody as young as you trying to keep people out of places. I mean, you expect it with older people. They get like that. But I'd have thought that with a lovely place like this for swimming you'd have been glad to let people come in and enjoy themselves.'

'I see,' said Celia. 'And, as you were just going to say, it doesn't really make any difference to me.'

'That's right,' said Ril, surprised. 'Yes, that's what I was going to say.'

'People are always saying it,' said Celia. 'Yesterday I had a letter from a man in Hallersage I've never met, wanting a hundred pounds to save his shop from closing. After all, what's a hundred pounds to Celia Withens? If I get a job done at Withishall I'm charged twice what anyone would pay in the town. After all, I can afford it. If anyone wants to start a subscription list for anything from a parish hall to a lost dogs' home they come to me. After all, I've got plenty.'

'Well, you *have* got plenty, haven't you?' said Ril. 'I

mean, isn't the sort of thing you're talking about simply the penalty for being rich?'

'You're not rich, are you?' inquired Celia.

Ril thought of her father's leather-patched jackets and the decrepit car Daisy.

'No such luck,' she said.

'And I expect you sleep well.'

Norman broke in rudely.

'Come off it!' he said. 'Being rich doesn't stop you sleepin'. Or, if it does, the answer's in your own hands. Give it all away an' get a job. That's what I'd do.'

Celia smiled.

'You wouldn't really,' she said. 'You think you would, but you wouldn't.'

'I would!' declared Norman with spirit.

'Well, I wouldn't,' said Ril. 'I'd never leave a house that had been in the family for generations. And I'd love to have lots of money. But I'd give most of it for schools and hospitals and scholarships for people from abroad and things like that. The Ril Terry Hospital. The Ril Terry Foundation. The Ril Terry all-sorts-of-things. I'd have a wonderful time.'

It occurred to her that it might be possible to turn the conversation to practical use.

'And if I owned this estate,' she went on, 'I'd just keep a little bit of garden round the house and I'd hand all the rest over to the public.'

'Oh God,' said Celia. She yawned. 'Don't start lecturing me about public spirit and all that. I've been hearing it since I was so high. And it always means the same thing. Somebody trying to get something out of me.'

'They don't have much luck, do they?' said Ril. 'What you have you hold.'

'You've been reading the motto. No, they don't have much luck. They think that because I'm a woman I must be a fool. And that annoys me. So I show them I'm not.'

85

Celia Withens lit a third cigarette from the stub of the second.

'Yes,' she went on, 'it's the feeling that people are trying to make a fool of you that hurts. That, and knowing they're only interested in you for what you've got, not what you are. If you two youngsters have friends at least you can assume that they like you. But if I have friends I don't know whether they like me or not.'

Ril was surprised.

'Fancy thinking of that!' she said. 'If it was me I'd just suppose they did like me. Anyway, can't you tell?'

'You can be wrong,' said Celia. 'At least, I've been wrong.'

She continued, talking half to herself:

'There was someone I thought liked me enormously, but it turned out that it wasn't that at all.'

'I'm sorry,' said Ril. 'Still, you must have plenty of friends, really. After all, you have everything, and you've been to all kinds of places, and you've lived abroad. . . .'

'My dear child,' said Celia, 'there's no special magic about living abroad. It doesn't help you to keep friends: quite the reverse. Shall I tell you something? I'm here at Withishall for a month, and there's no one I really want to have here with me. There are plenty who'd be glad to come, of course. . . .'

'But you'd be wondering what they were after?'

'I suppose so. Silly, isn't it?'

Celia, suddenly bored, got up. 'Off you go now,' she said, 'and if you come here again don't be caught.'

'I'm sorry,' said Ril, and offered her hand. Something in her expression appealed to Celia, who softened and added on impulse:

'But you can come here officially if you like. It'll be safer, though possibly duller. Why don't you both come to tea with me? Come tomorrow – no, the day after – at four.'

'Oh, I'd love to!' cried Ril eagerly. 'We'll come, won't we, Norman?'

'You can if you like,' said Norman gruffly. 'Not me. No offence meant, Miss Withens, but it's not in my line.'

And he refused to be persuaded.

'I think you were rude,' Ril told him when they were outside the wall. 'At least you could have made an excuse.'

'I speak my mind,' said Norman. 'I reckon nowt to excuses. What would I be doin' gettin' mixed up wi' folk like her?'

'You're stubborn!' Ril declared. 'I've never met anyone so unbudgeable.'

Norman took this as a compliment.

'Aye, I'm not easily shifted,' he said with a touch of complacency.

Ril had the urge to puncture him with a sharp word, but restrained herself. Instead she threw her rolled-up towel at him.

'Catch!' she called.

She knew he hadn't time. It hit him neatly in the face.

Ril ran.

'Ril, do you mind?' said Robert. 'I've asked Miss Sadler to supper tonight. I'm afraid it's short notice, but could you make something nice?'

'Of course,' said Ril. 'Give me some extra money and leave it to me.'

A thought crept into her mind.

'Miss Sadler's rather attractive, isn't she, Daddy?'

'Now, don't be silly,' said Robert. 'She's coming on business – to talk about a lecture course.'

'Oh dear, my romantic hopes dashed!' said Ril. 'Never mind. I don't think I want to share you.'

'Let me finish what I was saying. It'll be a deadly dull evening for you. So I wonder if you'd like to ask someone your own age as well. Then you needn't sit and listen to the old fogies. What about Norman?'

'What, ask Norman to spend an evening with a head-mistress? Goodness, he'd run a mile. No, I'll have to think of somebody else.'

Ril pondered for a moment and went on:

'I'd rather like to ask Hilda Woodward.'

'Do I know her?' asked Robert. Then, remembering, 'Oh yes, the spotty girl with glasses who looked after us on Speech Day.'

'She's a bit spotty,' Ril admitted. 'But I liked her. The trouble is, I don't know where she lives.'

'Ring the school secretary,' suggested Robert, on an un-usually practical note.

Ril did so, and learned that Hilda's address was 14, Milton Street. There was no telephone number. She got out the street-map and found that Milton Street was not far from Old Hallersage Road, on the way into town. She decided to go to Hallersage market to get something for the supper, and to call at Milton Street on the way. The thought was in her mind that her father, Miss Sadler, and Hilda would be the best available brains-trust to find the meaning (if any) in Caradoc Clough's message.

The weather was still hot, and it seemed to get hotter as Ril tramped towards the city centre. Trams groaned past. A long stretch of road was up, and the noise of pneumatic drills rattled her eardrums. Streams of heavy traffic crawled and hooted and changed gear and threw out exhaust fumes. The air was stale, tasting of soot and dustbins. Her feet ached on the endless pavement. Ril longed to be up on the moors or swimming in cool water.

The street-map had told her where Milton Street was, but hadn't told her what it was like. To turn into the side-streets was to enter a different world. Behind the Old Hallersage Road lay a tangle of little blackened stone houses: scores and scores of them, huddled into a maze of streets and courts. The district was on a slope, and there was a view across the hazy depths of the town to another house-laden slope a mile or so away. As Ril walked along Milton Street there was a thundery sound and the ground shook under her feet. She realized that the street was just above the main railway line.

Ril knocked at the door of No. 14 with misgivings. Like the rest of its row, the house had obviously not been painted for years. The stone step was hollow where generations of feet had trod. The doorknob was loose and the knocker broken. But the curtains were bright and contemporary.

She was startled when the door was opened by Sylvie, whom she had met at the dance-hall the previous weekend. Sylvie was just as surprised to see her; and not, Ril thought, especially pleased.

''Ullo!' she said. 'We're honoured, aren't we?'

'I wonder if I've come to the wrong house,' said Ril. 'I'm looking for Hilda Woodward.'

'Why, what's she done?'

'She hasn't done anything that I know of. I wanted to see her, that's all.'

'Oh. Well, you're at t'right 'ouse. I'm 'er sister. Fancy wantin' to see our 'Ilda. You'd better come in.'

The door opened straight into the living-room. It was a staggering contrast to the broken-down appearance of the outside. The room was well furnished, carpeted and cheerful. Ril noticed gay wallpaper, a tank of tropical fish, and an enormous instrument combining radio, television, and gramophone which was now emitting cheerful noises. A girl a year or two older than Sylvie was doing something to her hair in front of the looking-glass. And bustling in from the kitchen came a fat shapeless happy mother, big enough to make the solid Florrie seem in recollection like a model.

'Come right in, love!' she shouted, wiping her hands on her apron. 'Make yourself at 'ome. Whose pal are you?'

'She came to see 'Ilda,' said Sylvie; and then, suspiciously: 'So she says.'

''Ilda!' repeated Mrs Woodward. 'Our 'Ilda! Did you 'ear that, Janet? She's come to see our 'Ilda.'

Janet turned from the glass. She was a pretty blonde girl, very like Sylvie, but without Sylvie's thin face and sharp eye.

'Say 'ow do to t'young lady!' ordered Mrs Woodward.

''Ow do,' said Janet obediently. She turned back to the mirror, through which she continued to observe Ril with some interest.

'There's no need to call 'er t'young lady,' remarked Sylvie. 'She 'as a name, just like t'rest of us. If you can pronounce it, that is.'

'Aye, tell us your name, love,' said Mrs Woodward. 'No, let me guess. Summat fancy, is it? Dawn? Marilyn?' She took a deep breath. 'Mirabelle?'

'Nay, it's dafter than any o' those,' said Sylvie.

'Now, now, where's your manners?' demanded Mrs Woodward. 'It's not for you to say what's daft. There was a few that 'ad summat to say when we called you Sylvie, I can tell you.'

'Don't bother about my full name,' Ril said hastily. 'Just call me Ril.'

''Er name,' said Sylvie deliberately, 'is Amaryllis.'

'Amaryllis!' shouted Mrs Woodward. She was delighted. 'Amaryllis! It's a lovely name!'

'Roy thinks so,' said Sylvie. There was a grim note in her voice. 'Roy thinks she's t'cat's whiskers. So superior. Charmed, may dear Amaryllis, ay'm sure.'

'I don't know what's come over you, our Sylvie!' declared Mrs Woodward. 'She isn't usually like this, love. Tek no notice of 'er. She's a bit upset about summat.'

Janet now spoke at last.

'She came to see 'Ilda,' she pointed out, 'not to argue about names.'

'Oh aye, of course,' said Mrs Woodward. 'Our 'Ilda's stuck in a book, I expect.' She went to the stairs and bellowed: ''Ilda-a-a! 'Ilda-a-a!'

A voice from above responded faintly.

'She'll be down in a minute, duck,' Mrs Woodward announced. 'I'll just be makin' a cupper tea. Nay, it's no bother, you'll 'ave to 'ave a cupper tea while you're 'ere. Anyroad, I'm parched myself.'

She disappeared into the kitchen, followed by Janet. Sylvie and Ril faced each other.

'Did you really come to see 'Ilda?' asked Sylvie in a low voice.

Ril nodded.

'I thought it might 'a' been summat to do wi' Roy.'

'I hardly know Roy,' said Ril.

'But you're interested in 'im, aren't you?'

'No, I'm not,' said Ril with a touch of impatience, 'and I've no reason to think he's interested in me. I haven't seen him since that night at the Rex.'

'All right,' said Sylvie. 'Never mind. But if 'e isn't after you 'e'll be after somebody else. 'E's tired of me, the so-and-so!'

The room was noisily invaded by Mrs Woodward, carrying a big tin tray and followed by a nondescript dog, which in turn was pursued by Janet with a lead. Hilda's silent appearance at the other door was unnoticed for a moment. Then her mother and sisters all turned on her at once.

'Eh, just look at t'lass!' exclaimed Mrs Woodward, vexed.

Hilda was no delight to the eye. Unlike any other girl

during school holidays, she was still wearing uniform, and a crumpled uniform at that. Her spectacles glinted and her spots were all too obvious. Beyond running a comb through her hair she had done nothing to make herself presentable. In spite of the fine weather she was pale and had obviously not been out of doors much.

Janet and Sylvie sighed at each other.

'Makes you weep, dun't it?' said Sylvie.

'Eh, 'Ilda love,' protested Mrs Woodward. 'Do you 'ave to look like that when folks call?'

'Or any other time?' said Janet.

'I can't help the way I look,' said Hilda sullenly. 'We can't all be Helen of Troy, can we? Hullo, Ril.'

Like Sylvie, she seemed less than welcoming.

Ril had intended to offer her invitation to Hilda privately. But there was no question of that. Mrs Woodward and the two older girls crowded round, eager to know what it was all about.

'I just wondered if you could come to supper with us to-night,' Ril said to Hilda.

''Course she can!' declared Mrs Woodward ''Course she can! Do 'er a world o' good to get out for once. You wouldn't believe it, t'way this lass stops at 'ome. It's easy to see she's t'grammar-school one in this 'ouse. Never goes to t'pictures, never goes to no dances . . .'

'All right, all right, Mum,' said Hilda crossly, 'spare us the gory details.' She turned to Ril. 'Thank you very much,' she said formally. 'It's nice of you to ask me.'

Ril thought she had better make the set-up clear.

'Miss Sadler's coming,' she said. 'She has to talk business with my father. So he thought it would be nice if someone of my own age came too.'

'And you thought of our 'Ilda!' said Janet wonderingly.

'Well, it was right nice of you . . .' began Mrs Woodward; and then the light dawned.

'Miss Sadler!' she repeated. 'That's t'head teacher at t'school!'

Ril nodded.

The two older girls rolled their eyes at each other.

'Just t'job for our 'Ilda, I should think,' remarked Sylvie. 'They can 'ave a nice chat about Latin grammar.'

Hilda looked nervous.

'Now, leave t'lass alone, our Sylvie!' ordered Mrs Woodward. 'It'll be a right nice outin' for 'er. I don't know what she'll wear, though. She can't go lookin' like that.'

'I can go in my uniform,' said Hilda. 'I'll press it up first.'

'No-o-o-o!' said the other three all together.

Hilda looked at Ril appealingly.

'It's not a special occasion,' Ril said. 'I shall just wear a summer frock myself.'

''Ilda 'asn't got owt fit to wear,' said Sylvie, 'an' it's 'er own fault. She can't be bothered. It 'ardly seems natural to me.'

'Well, you don't think of anything else!' snapped Hilda. 'I've got other things on my mind.'

'Books,' said Sylvie pityingly.

'Well, I bet Ril reads books,' said Janet. 'But she dun't look a mess like our 'Ilda.'

'Leave t'lass alone!' said Mrs Woodward once more. 'Now 'Ilda, I'll give you some money. Three pound, 'ow's that? Go down to t'shops an' get yourself a nice frock. Janet, can't you or Sylvie go along an' see she gets summat that suits 'er?'

The two girls pulled faces at each other.

'Can I help?' asked Ril. 'I've got to go into town, anyway.'

Mrs Woodward beamed.

'Now that really would be nice!' she said. 'You go along with 'er, Ril love. Seems funny for a lass of 'er age, but it's like Sylvie said. She's never 'ad no interest in clothes. Go on, 'Ilda, off you go. Don't keep your pal waitin'.'

As they went out Janet turned the radio up.

*

'What did you come here for?' demanded Hilda furiously when she and Ril were outside.

Ril stared.

'But you know why,' she said.

'Well, haven't you any imagination? When you got to Milton Street couldn't you have guessed? I felt so ashamed having you in there, I could have died.'

'What's wrong with me?' asked Ril indignantly.

'I don't mean you. I mean them. I wouldn't have had you meet them for worlds.'

'Your mother and sisters? I liked meeting them. I'd met Sylvie before, as a matter of fact.'

'But they're – oh, they're impossible!'

'Your mother's nice.'

'She means well but she doesn't understand. What she'd really like is for me to be just like them. A pair of feather-brains without a thought in their heads but dates and make-up and pop-tunes and . . .'

'They're pretty, aren't they?' said Ril. 'And I wouldn't call Sylvie featherbrained. Or Janet either, I daresay. I should think you could get on with them if you met them halfway.'

'Meet them halfway!' echoed Hilda. 'I wish I needn't meet them at all. Oh, if only I could get out of that place. They're all so – so illiterate!'

'I bet it's a cheerful place to live,' said Ril. 'I live with my father. I'd like to have a couple of sisters to brighten things up.'

'I'll swap you,' offered Hilda.

Ril's thoughts were on another track.

'It's funny,' she said, 'there's my cousin Norman all steamed up in case he gets separated from the people and

94

ways he's used to. And here are you all steamed up because you don't like your own background.'

'And what about you?' asked Hilda.

'I don't seem to have any background,' Ril said ruefully. 'I don't belong to Belhampton any more. And I don't belong here. Maybe I'll never belong anywhere again.'

Hilda had gradually calmed down. Now she changed the subject.

'I'll be scared of Miss Sadler,' she said. 'Whatever will we talk to her about?'

'I can think of something,' said Ril. 'I've got a sort of puzzle that's bothering me. If we all tackle it together we might be able to solve it.'

'I won't dare say a word,' said Hilda. 'I shall just open and shut my mouth like a fish, and nothing will come out.'

'Rubbish,' said Ril. 'Now, come along. I've got to go to the market, and then we've to buy you a dress. What shall we look for?'

'Oh, don't you start!' said Hilda. 'Any old thing will do.'

Ril pulled a face at the nearest wall. She felt a good deal of sympathy with Janet and Sylvie. Three pounds to spend, and so little interest in the matter. As Sylvie had said, it hardly seemed natural. . .

'The secret of good cooking,' said Ril, 'is not to cook at all if you can help it.'

She was showing off a little for Hilda's benefit. And certainly the meal she had provided for Miss Sadler's visit had been a success on a hot evening: cold consommé, salmon salad and fruit. Now the two girls were washing up and giggling a little together.

Hilda's three pounds had provided a pair of gay sandals as well as a summer frock, and Ril had helped her to do her hair. A compliment from Miss Sadler had raised her morale considerably. By now she was enjoying herself.

From the sitting-room came the sounds of friendly talk and occasional laughter. Robert and Miss Sadler were engaged on the business of the evening: discussion of a lecture course on social history.

'He said it would be deadly dull,' Ril confided to Hilda, 'but it seems to be keeping them amused.'

'Ought we to make the washing-up last a bit longer?'

'Goodness, no, we don't have to do that. I want to try them with my conundrum.'

They returned to the sitting-room. The timing, as it happened, was perfect.

'We were thinking,' said Robert, 'of having a talk on the old order in the countryside, and how the growth of the new industrial towns affected it.'

'As in Hallersage, for instance?' asked Ril.

'Yes, indeed. We like to bring in local associations. It keeps people interested.'

'Oh well, I've been doing a bit of research on that myself,' Ril announced. ('Research' sounded good, she thought.) 'I've been finding out about some of the things that followed Caradoc Clough's revolt.'

She told them in outline the story that Florrie had told her, concluding with the mysterious message she had been given by Aunt Martha.

As she finished Robert and Miss Sadler exchanged glances. Miss Sadler looked half impressed, half alarmed.

'If you're not careful,' she said, 'you'll be making a live issue out of all this.'

'Well, I want to,' said Ril. 'Hallersage could do to get the

Common back, couldn't it, Miss Sadler? Among other things we might get some playing-fields for the school.'

Miss Sadler sighed.

'We shan't get much out of Celia Withens,' she said.

'But the message,' said Ril. ' "It's not behind the *night thoughts*." If we knew what that meant we might really be on the track of something.'

'I hate to disillusion you,' said Robert, 'but I don't think it means anything at all. The wanderings of an old man, most likely. Or if it ever did mean something it's got all mixed up in being passed from mouth to mouth. It doesn't make any kind of sense to me.'

'Or to me, I'm afraid,' said Miss Sadler. 'No, Ril, you might as well forget it. . . .'

But at this point her voice trailed off. Watching her face, Ril could tell that a new thought had struck her. And looking across at Hilda she saw the same light dawning in Hilda's eye.

'Young !' they exclaimed together.

Ril was baffled. So, she could see, was her father.

'I'm afraid the Terrys aren't with you,' she said.

'Tell them, Hilda,' said Miss Sadler, smiling.

Hilda's eyes sparkled as she enjoyed an opportunity to shine.

'Edward Young,' she announced in textbook manner, 'lived from about 1680 to 1760. He wrote a long philosophical poem called *Night Thoughts*, which enjoyed great popularity in the late eighteenth and early nineteenth centuries. . . .'

'But which hasn't been heard of by me,' admitted Ril.

'Or by me,' said Robert. 'Does it make any sense out of the message?'

Hilda was now getting into top gear.

'I bet it means an actual book,' she declared. 'A copy of the *Night Thoughts*. With something hidden behind it.'

'But it says "Not behind the *Night Thoughts*",' Ril objected.

'I'd be inclined to forget the negative,' said Robert thoughtfully. 'That may have crept in by accident. I mean, why bother to say where something *isn't*? People usually say where something *is*.'

'Yes, of course!' exclaimed Hilda eagerly. 'You wouldn't bother to say *not* behind the *Night Thoughts* any more than you'd say *not* behind the Works of William Shakespeare.'

Ril was bewildered.

'Oh, don't drag Shakespeare into it!' she groaned.

Hilda looked at her pityingly. Earlier in the day she had felt inferior. Now the balance was being restored.

'Assuming we're right to ignore the "not",' continued Robert, 'what do we suppose is, or was, hidden behind a copy of the *Night Thoughts*?'

Ril recovered.

'A document returning Old Hallersage Common to the townspeople!' she cried.

Robert and Miss Sadler both smiled.

'Your daughter has a romantic imagination, Mr Terry,' said Miss Sadler.

To her horror, Ril felt herself blushing.

'Sorry, Ril,' said Miss Sadler. 'You could be right. No harm in hoping. The next question is, where was the copy of the *Night Thoughts* that the message refers to?'

Hilda jumped in again. She was having a wonderful time.

'The message was from Sir George Withens to Caradoc Clough,' she said. 'So it would be pretty certain to refer to Sir George's own copy of the book. And it would be in the library at Withishall.'

'Is there a library at Withishall?' asked Robert.

'Indeed there is,' said Miss Sadler.

There was a moment's silence. Hilda basked in the general admiration. Then:

'You may be right, Hilda,' said Miss Sadler. 'But if you are, I'm afraid there's no hope that anything will come of it now. If there was a document – or anything else – hidden behind a book it could hardly have stayed hidden for nearly a hundred years. It must have been found and presumably destroyed.'

The two girls' faces fell.

'I expect I shall see Celia Withens again before she leaves Hallersage,' said Miss Sadler. 'I'll ask her whether anything ever turned up. She might just know something about it. If she doesn't I'm afraid it's the end of the matter. Though the story Ril told us earlier on throws a bit more light on the subject of our lecture series. . . .'

And the conversation drifted back to business.

'You were pretty bright tonight, Hilda,' said Ril when they had a few minutes together at the end of the evening. 'Miss Sadler was impressed.'

Hilda looked almost dreamy.

'What a day !' she said. 'I bought a new dress, I went out to dinner, I shone in company – and you know what, Ril? Miss Sadler's running me home in her car.'

Ril was delighted by Hilda's pleasure and forgot her own failure to shine.

'Keep it up,' she urged. 'New horizons, Hilda.' She waved her arm round in a magnificent gesture. 'The richness of life lies before you. . . .'

'Shut up,' said Hilda. She was thoughtful again now.

'All the same,' she went on, 'I shall ask Miss Sadler to drop me at the corner of the main road. I'm not taking her into Milton Street.'

'I think that's silly,' said Ril.

'It's not silly at all,' said Hilda.

She took off her spectacles and wiped them. She'd powdered over her spots, but they were showing through again.

*

'I've got a bone to pick wi' you,' said Norman.

'Pick away,' said Roy affably.

'That car you sold for three 'undred in cash today . . .'

'Well?'

'Well, it's still on 'ire-purchase.'

'So what?'

'If t'payments wasn't kept up t'company could take it back. Then what'd t'poor chap who bought it do?'

'Don't worry. I'll keep up the payments.'

'Why don't you settle the account like you told the seller you would? After all, you've got t'cash. You only paid 'im the difference when you bought t'car.'

'I need capital, lad. I always need capital.'

'It's not straight, Roy, that's t'long an' short of it. An' then there's that old crock you sold yesterday. Sawdust in t'gearbox – that's a rotten old trick. An' resprayed one coat over t'top of all that rust.'

'Now listen, lad. I pay you to work on cars, not to lecture me on business morality. Give it a rest, will you?'

'I will in a minute. But what about that Morris over there? It 'ad sixty thousand miles on t'clock when it came in. It's only got twenty-two thousand now.'

'If every dealer who's turned the clock back was laid end to end they'd reach from here to Detroit,' said Roy.

'An' then there's that Vauxhall . . .'

'Stuff it, Norman, will you? I'm not in the mood.'

'All right, I'm not lecturin' you. I'm just tellin' you these last few days when I've been workin' nearly full time 'ave opened my eyes. If you don't do your business on t'level you can count me out of it.'

Roy laughed.

'You don't know you're born,' he said. 'Wait till you've seen a real trick or two.'

'I don't want to, thank you.'

'Then you'd better keep away from the car trade.'

'I'll keep away from your bit of it, anyroad. I'm packin' it in, Roy.'

'What about the motor-bike you were saving for?'

'Don't worry. I can easy get work. Easier than you'll get a mechanic.'

Roy laughed again.

'I had Ted Bellingham round yesterday looking for a job,' he said. 'I guess I'll give him one. It'll cost me more but Ted will stay. Being forty he won't be going back to school next month.'

Norman raised his eyes to heaven.

'Ted Bellingham!' he echoed. 'I wouldn't trust 'im to mend a kid's scooter. What with you an' 'im, I pity your customers!'

'You can stay if you like, lad,' said Roy with an air of generosity.

'Not on your terms, an' that's flat.'

A thought occurred to Roy.

'Has that nice little cousin of yours been getting at you?' he inquired. 'I shouldn't think she'd care for the car trade. Not gentlemanly enough.'

'She never said owt about it. She's all for my stayin' at school, though.'

'You won't keep up with her, lad, I can tell you. She'll be flying higher than you.'

'She could mix wi' t'nobs if she felt like it,' Norman admitted. 'You know what? She's goin' to tea wi' Miss Withens on Monday.'

'Is she now?' inquired Roy with interest.

'Aye, an' if you want to know, I could 'a' gone too. We met Miss Withens in – well, never mind. "Why don't you both come to tea on Monday at four?" she says. I turned it down, but Ril's goin'.'

'I told you, boy, she's cut out for higher things. She'll be pretending she doesn't know you soon.'

'Ril's all right,' said Norman shortly. 'Anyone that says she isn't, I'll bash them.'

'Tea for two,' mused Roy. He modulated into the show-room accent. 'Tea with the glorious, the incomparable, Celia. Oh, what a date of dates. And to have it wasted on a little schoolgirl!' He was silent for a moment. Then, returning to his manner:

'How will she get there, lad? It's a long way up to the hall. When you get to the gate you're still only halfway there.'

'She 'as a bike. She'll go on that.'

'She might be glad of a lift,' said Roy, half to himself.

He grinned cheerfully at Norman.

'Let's not part on bad terms, lad, eh? I owe you for an hour or two's work. Here's a quid. Never mind the change. And if you think better of it you can come back – I might find something for you to do. . . . Well, what are you waiting for?'

'It's twenty-four-an'-six you owe me,' said Norman.

10

Monday, the day Ril was to go to tea at Withishall, was the twelfth of the heat-wave. Even Robert had become conscious of the weather and was wearing an open-necked shirt and a pair of Army-surplus shorts which displayed his rather knobbly knees. Ril left him in mid-afternoon surrounded by lecture-notes and timetables.

'I've put out a tea-tray for you,' she told him.

'Yes, dear.'

'You only need to boil the kettle when the time comes.'

'Yes, dear.'

'Just plug it in to that power-point over the cooker.'

'Yes, dear.'

'I bet you'll forget, won't you?'

'Yes – no, dear.'

Ril sighed and went to fetch her bicycle. The heat hit her as soon as she wheeled it into the road. It was uphill all the way from Park Terrace: not steep enough to make cycling impossible but steep enough to make heavy going on a hot day.

She was just coming up to Old Hallersage market-place when she heard a motor-horn pip-pipping behind her. It was Roy in the Triumph.

Ril got off her machine, not sorry of the excuse for a minute's rest.

Roy drew in to the kerb. Ostentatiously he doffed his hat.

'Yes,' said Ril, 'it's the fair Amaryllis.'

Roy grinned, and opened the car door at the passenger side.

'Allow me,' he said in the showroom accent, 'to convey you to your destination.'

'Didn't you notice this?' asked Ril, pointing to the bicycle.

'Oh, leave it by the wayside,' said Roy airily. 'Unsuitable weather for that kind of sport.'

'How do you know you're going my way?'

'You are going,' said Roy, 'to take tea with Miss Celia Withens.'

'Did Norman tell you?'

'He did. I trust he was not indiscreet.'

'No, of course not. It isn't a secret. But –'

'It will be a pleasure to take you there.'

'You could only go to the gate,' Ril said, 'and I'd still have a long way to walk when I got inside.'

'Surely,' said Roy, 'I can drive Miss Withens's guest up to the house.'

'And are you doing all this just out of kindness to me?'

'I have a little natural curiosity, I admit,' said Roy. 'I shall enjoy a chance to drive through the park. Few of us have been as privileged as you are, my dear Amaryllis.'

Ril began to find his mannerisms tiresome.

'I wish you'd just call me Ril and talk to me naturally,' she said with a touch of impatience.

'Certainly, my dear Amaryllis,' said Roy, unperturbed.

'Anyway, thank you for offering me a lift, but I can't take it. I'll need the bike to get home again.'

'Not so,' said Roy. 'I shall call for you later on.' He looked at her guilelessly.

Ril hesitated. But it was very hot. Besides, she had nothing against Roy. He had got her out of difficulty at the Rex and had delivered her safely home.

'Well, I could leave the bike at Cousin Florrie's,' she said. 'It's just round the corner, in the market-place. I'll tell her you're giving me a lift.'

It took only a minute to deposit the bicycle with Florrie. When Ril came out of the house Roy and the Triumph were waiting for her. Soon they were soaring up the Withishall Road. In such heat the rush of wind and the speed of the car were exhilarating.

At the Withens gate Roy drew up and pip-pipped again. An old woman put her head out of the lodge door.

'Miss Terry, to see Miss Withens,' announced Roy.

Without a word the old woman opened the gate. They drove through the park, with the Triumph throwing up a cloud of white dust from the unsurfaced road.

The road ran first through a spinney and then across flat land which must have been part of the old Common. Then it crossed the river and swept in a straight line towards the house.

Ril looked at Withishall with interest as they approached. Basically it was an austere stone-built classical house of medium size, but a disproportionately large portico had been added at the front and other additions had been made at various times, rather spoiling the outline. From somewhere at the back, with its lower part hidden, rose a peculiar, vaguely-medieval bell-tower.

The Triumph drew up with a flourish at the steps of the portico. Courteously Roy handed his passenger out. The main door of the house was closed. To Ril's disappointment it stayed closed, but almost at once Miss Withens appeared at a much smaller door a few yards along. She was wearing a yellow jumper and a tweed skirt, and still managing to look remarkably elegant.

'Hullo, Ril,' she said. 'I wondered if you'd come. I'm glad you did.' And then, looking at Roy :

'Who's the friend?'

Roy half bowed, and swept the air with his hat in an ex-aggerated gesture.

'This is Mr...' Ril began, and realized with horror that she had never heard Roy's surname.

'Wentworth,' said Roy easily. 'Roy Wentworth.'

'Mr Wentworth kindly drove me here,' said Ril un-necessarily.

Celia and Roy exchanged looks. Celia's expression was cool, quizzical, half amused. Roy's was of unconcealed ad-miration.

'But how nice of Mr Wentworth,' said Celia.

'It was a pleasure, Miss Withens,' said Roy. He smiled, showing his perfect teeth. 'It will be an equal pleasure to return for her at a suitable hour.'

'Have you come up from Hallersage, Mr Wentworth?' inquired Celia.

Roy nodded.

'It seems a shame for you to go away and come back again,' said Celia. 'Unless you have business to do, of course. . . .'

'There's always business, isn't there?' said Roy. 'Though sometimes one neglects it.'

'If you're able to neglect yours,' said Celia, 'perhaps you could stay to tea with Ril and myself?'

Roy bowed.

'That would be delightful,' he said.

Inwardly he was triumphant. This was what he had hoped for but hadn't dared to expect. The invitation had been offered only out of politeness, but still it wouldn't have been offered at all if he hadn't made a reasonably good first impression. Roy congratulated himself on the good looks, the good clothes, and the showroom accent. They had served him well. Here was he, Roy Wentworth, born in a Hallersage back-street, and now about to take tea with the rich and beautiful Celia Withens. Even if he never saw her again it would be something to boast about. And you never knew . . .

Ril guessed nothing of Roy's thoughts. She felt a sudden romantic excitement. Here was poor Celia, she thought, probably getting tired by now of her own company. And here was Roy, undeniably handsome; and his friendship with Sylvie didn't seem to be working out. Suppose an attachment were to grow up between them? . . . It would be like a modern fairy-tale: the heiress and the car salesman.

Some of Norman's remarks about Roy occurred to her, but she dismissed them. Norman, she decided, was altogether too cynical.

*

A middle-aged housekeeper brought in the tea. With her husband (nominally butler but in reality no more than a handyman), and a young girl and a cleaning-woman, she was all that remained of the indoor staff of Withishall. When, after tea, Celia took her guests round the house, the neglect was obvious. Though not on stately home scale,

Withishall was too much for four people to look after. In many rooms the furniture was covered with dust-sheets. Celia herself occupied only a little of the ground floor.

Ril's heart thumped when they came to the library. Here, possibly, lay the document referred to by Caradoc Clough in the message passed on by Great-Aunt Martha.

The room was high and chilling, with three classical figures on pedestals, and hundreds of feet of shelving built into the walls. There were thousands of leather-bound volumes, many of them unidentifiable from the spines. One of these might well be the *Night Thoughts* – but if so it could take days to find it.

'Are any of these ever read?' she asked Celia.

'Not by me,' Celia said. 'I keep my own books in my own quarters. You wouldn't come in here to read a modern novel or a paperback, would you?'

'So they just sit here, year in, year out?'

Celia nodded.

Ril felt a faint hope rise within her.

'And could some of the books have been in the same place for a hundred years?' she asked.

Celia stared.

'What an odd question,' she said. And then: 'No, I'm sure they haven't. My grandfather used to rearrange them from time to time.'

'He was a book-lover, I suppose?' said Roy.

'Not in the least,' said Celia. 'I don't think any of the Withenses were book-lovers. To my grandfather the books were part of the furniture. In the end he put them in order of size. You see how they go – from big books at the ends of the shelves to little ones in the middle. That's the only kind of order they're in.'

Ril groaned. There could hardly be any system that would make it harder to find a single book. Still, she was not giving up at once.

'Do you know if there's a copy of Young's *Night Thoughts?*' she asked.

'Never heard of it,' said Celia casually. 'I don't really know what there is. I don't think anybody knows.'

A thought now struck Roy.

'But there might be something rare,' he said. 'Something valuable.'

'There might,' said Celia, 'but I doubt it. Other families collected books and paintings, but the Withenses just accumulated junk. No taste.' She smiled faintly. 'Even so, the insurance company are always going on at me to have everything valued, just as they're always going on at me to have burglar-alarms fitted. I suppose one of these days I'll have to stay at Withishall long enough to get everything organized. But I'm afraid it soon palls.'

'It all seems a strange setting for a beautiful young lady,' said Roy sententiously. He switched on the admiring look again. Celia gave him a quizzical glance but said nothing.

'I'll take you to see the bell-tower now,' she said. 'Most people seem to find it the most interesting thing in the house. It was built by my great-great-grandfather Sir George Withens. He was the fourth baronet. I call him George the Fourth.'

Ril pricked up her ears. This was the man who had sent Caradoc Clough to Australia.

From the library Celia took them to the far end of the east wing. At one time this would have been the end of the house, but now there was a little doorway leading into the bell-tower. Inside was nothing but a spiral stone staircase. There were slits in the walls, through which Ril caught glimpses of green trees or blue sky.

At the top of the staircase they emerged into a round room, wider in diameter than the lower part of the tower. It was musty and gloomy and contained nothing but a writing-desk, a table, and a cupboard – old, dusty, and full of wormholes. Near the writing-desk a rope hung down from the roof. It was some time before Ril realized that this was the tuft of the bell-rope.

'Now here's a place that probably *has* been unaltered for a hundred years,' said Celia. 'This was George the Fourth's private den. He came here to do the accounts and so on. He was an odd, secretive old chap, so far as I can gather. He had all this built for himself.'

'It seems an elaborate way of providing yourself with a study,' said Ril, puzzled.

'Oh, he didn't do it just for that. I think the study was really a by-product. The bell was the thing. Come and look at it.'

An iron ladder led up to the tiny gallery that surrounded the bell-frame. As they stepped into the open air Ril felt suddenly dizzy, and had to grip the railings. They were eighty feet above the ground, and the rest of Withishall lay below them.

Ril stood blinking in the strong sunlight. When she recovered she walked slowly round the gallery, taking in the view. On three sides the high hills rolled away into the distance. On the fourth side lay most of the Withens estate, and beyond it the spires and chimneys of Hallersage, fading eventually into the smoke-haze.

'I'm afraid old George the Fourth didn't build it for the view,' said Celia. 'It was a few years after the French Revolution, when all the old squires were scared stiff that something of the sort might happen here. This was meant as a watch-tower and if necessary a stronghold in case of revolt. And the bell was to be rung as a warning and a call for help.'

'What a curious idea!' said Roy.

'Well, I believe they'd just had some kind of peasants' rising in Hallersage,' said Celia. 'It didn't come to anything, though.'

'Obviously,' said Roy, 'since the Withens family is still so stoutly entrenched.'

'The Withens family,' said Celia on a slightly grim note, 'is me. The end of the line.'

Ril was looking at the bell. It was big, rusty, and rather frightening.

'Does it still ring?' she asked.

'It's supposed to be serviceable,' said Celia. 'They rang it for my twenty-first birthday. For heaven's sake don't try it – you'll frighten the household and probably bring the fire brigade.'

Ril looked over the railings again.

'It's fascinating up here, isn't it?' she said.

'I suppose so,' said Celia. She and Roy were getting bored. 'You can stay and look round for a few minutes if you like, Ril. But watch yourself on those steps when you go down. And whatever you do, don't fall over the railings or we shall have a nasty mess on the drive.'

Celia and Roy disappeared. Ril, still feeling romantic, decided to leave them to themselves for a while. Besides, she had permission to 'look round'. As a guest in Celia's house she could hardly have prowled about without asking. But she could interpret her permission liberally. She took it to include the room that had been George the Fourth's den, and after a minute or two she descended to it from the gallery.

Surely it would do no harm to look inside that ancient writing-desk. Ril pulled the top drawer out quickly, before her conscience had time to protest. And there was an immediate find : a wooden box containing a yellowed ivory set of dominoes. These were probably the very dominoes with which Sir George had played against Caradoc in his later years. Ril handled two or three of them with awe, then remembered that she had not much time and hurriedly replaced them.

After that exciting start came disappointment. All the drawers were empty. Ril moved over to the cupboard. The upper shelves of that were empty, too. In the bottom of the cupboard was a jumble of books and papers. She pulled them all out, getting her hands black, and choking with the dust that rose from them. But there were no wills, no codicils, nothing that appeared to be of the slightest value.

The books were account-books, with details in faded ink of all kinds of expenditure. Ril made a mental note to mention them to her father, in case they were of interest for his social history. The documents were nearly all letters addressed to Sir George. It was hard to tell who they were from or what they were about. After trying to read two or three she gave it up. At the very bottom of the cupboard was a biggish book which seemed to contain a household inventory. It recorded items of furniture, carpets, plate, and so on, room by room. Ril barely glanced at it before putting it back.

She had piled a few of the papers on top of it when a thought crossed her mind. She groped for the book again. With sudden excitement she flicked through the pages. Yes, the library! The three classical figures were listed (they had cost Sir George five pounds each). Four armchairs. An inkstand. A silver paperknife with jade handle. And then, sprawling over many pages, was a list of books. They were listed shelf by shelf, each shelf being numbered. And at the front was a diagram showing which shelf was indicated by each number.

But the list of titles was hard to read. The handwriting was crabbed and the ink had faded. And the list went on for page after page. It would take a long time to locate the *Night Thoughts*, if indeed it was listed at all.

Ril wondered whether to ask Celia to lend her the inventory. That would mean explaining what she was up to, which would be embarrassing. On the other hand, she could hardly go much further without telling Celia anyway. Pondering the problem, she turned over a few pages, each with its two or three columns of titles. What patience Sir George must have had to compile such a record! Ril imagined the eccentric old man, locked away in his study, filling the long days with all this pointless documentation, and looking forward perhaps to a game of dominoes with his old enemy in the evening.

It was then that she had her stroke of luck. The pages settled open – perhaps because of a little extra use – at the place where a single entry had been marked with a cross at each end in different ink. Ril peered at it. And yes, unbelievably, it was the one:

22.6 Young, Ed^{wd}. Night Tho^{ts}.

*

The discovery filled Ril with elation: not so much because of the find itself as because it was a clear sign that the *Night Thoughts* really did have some special significance. Until now there had been nothing to go on except Hilda's guess, which might not have been on the right track at all. Yet somebody, presumably the owner of the inventory, had gone to the trouble to mark this entry so he could easily find it.

The next step was to find the place in the library itself. Ril turned back to the diagram. The *Night Thoughts* was – or had been – the sixth book on Shelf 22. She made a rapid sketch in her diary of the part of the key that showed where this shelf was. Then she pushed the documents back into the cupboard, hurried down the spiral stair, and let herself into the main part of the house.

Ril was getting worried about the time. It was nearly six. Celia and Roy had left her half an hour ago. Any minute now somebody might come looking for her.

But the corridor that led past the library was empty. The

temptation was too much. Ril slipped through the library door and closed it behind her. The shelves were no longer numbered, but from her copy of the key she could tell quite easily which had been Shelf 22. It was to the left of the door, at the very top.

A pair of library steps stood near by. Ril climbed up. The shelf was not locked. She took out the first half-dozen books. And now once more came disappointment. The sixth book was not the *Night Thoughts*, nor were any of those near it; and behind them was only the bare panelling. She had drawn a blank.

There was no time to look any further. Rapidly she replaced the books, put the library steps back where they had been, and slipped out into the corridor. A minute later she rejoined Celia and Roy in the little downstairs room where they had all taken tea.

'Heavens!' cried Celia. 'Just look at the child! Ril, whatever have you been doing? You can't go home like that. Go and have a wash – second door on the right.'

Ril fumed. To be called a child and sent for a wash! She felt an illogical resentment against Celia. But it faded in the last few minutes of her visit. Celia asked her about Nightingales and about her feelings on leaving the South; and went on to talk of the contrast in her own life between the villa on the Riviera and grey northern Withishall. She seemed more animated, and perhaps happier, than when she and Ril had first met.

'You must come again before I leave,' she said finally; though whether to Ril or Roy or both was not quite clear.

As they drove away in the Triumph Roy was whistling.

'I think you made a good impression,' said Ril encouragingly.

'I think I did,' he agreed with satisfaction.

'Miss Withens is rather nice, isn't she? But not easy to know.'

'I'll get to know her. I mean to take her up on that invitation.'

Clearly Roy had assumed that it was meant for him.

*

'And how's Aunt Martha?' Ril asked when she went to collect her bicycle from Cousin Florrie's.

Florrie's face clouded.

'She's bin a bit restless lately,' she said. 'It's partly t'heat, I suppose. An' she's bin dreamin', an' all. She dreamed t'Withis'all bell rang out, an' she says that means trouble for t'Cloughs.'

'Shall I go and see her?'

'I wouldn't do that, love. Not just now. Come again when she's more settled.'

'I hope I haven't unsettled her.'

'Nay, love, she's better in lots o' ways since she saw you. She seems to 'ave taken more interest in life, like. All t'same, I wish I 'adn't . . .'

Florrie's voice trailed away.

'I've just come from Withishall now,' said Ril.

'Oh aye,' said Florrie. She spoke without enthusiasm.

'And I had tea with Miss Withens.'

'Oh aye?'

'She's very beautiful, isn't she?'

'So they tell me,' said Florrie.

'I saw an old box of dominoes. Probably the very ones that Sir George and Caradoc played with.'

'Ril,' began Florrie on a troubled note. 'Ril, there's summat . . .' She wiped her hands nervously on her apron and began again. 'Fred wants to see you. 'E's just come 'ome from work. Sit there, an' I'll give 'im a shout.'

She called through the kitchen door, and a minute later Fred came in. He was holding the towel on which he had just dried his face, and though he didn't realize it he was

114

still wearing his bicycle clips. And he was embarrassed.

'Ril, lass,' he began, in the dogged tone of a man who has something to say and means to go through with it, 'I want you to drop all this Caradoc business. Florrie 'ad no right to tell you what she did, or to let you get talkin' to Aunt Martha. An' now I 'ear you've bin up at Withis'all. Well, this is nowt to do wi' you, do you see? If it's to do wi' anybody it's to do wi' t'Cloughs, an' I told you before that we don't want to go stirrin' it up.'

'I'm a Clough myself,' said Ril obstinately.

'You're nobbut a bit o' one,' said Fred. 'T'real Cloughs is them that 'ave lived 'ere all their lives, an' there's none o' them wants to tamper wi' this. An' it's not right that a young lass like you should come up 'ere from t'other end o' t'country an' start pokin' your nose in.'

Florrie saw the mutinous look on Ril's face.

''E means it, love,' she said earnestly. 'That's quite a speech for 'im, you know.'

'I don't see what harm I can do,' said Ril.

'There's a load o' trouble wrapped up in it,' said Fred.

Ril looked appealingly at Norman, who had just come into the room.

'You'll never put 'er off by tellin' 'er not to meddle,' said Norman to his parents. 'It's not in 'er nature. She's as stubborn as they come.' He spoke in the tone of one paying a compliment.

'She'll 'appen do what 'er dad tells 'er,' said Fred.

Ril glared.

'Eh, let's not bother 'er dad about it,' said Florrie.

'I reckon we're all makin' too much fuss about it altogether,' said Norman. 'Now, Dad, I'll walk 'ome wi' Ril. I've got summat to suggest to 'er that'll clear it all up wi'out worryin' anybody. You leave it to me.'

Fred and Florrie looked doubtfully at each other.

'Eh, t'young folks these days . . .' began Florrie.

'Well, give t'lad a chance,' said Fred. He had screwed himself up to the point of speaking to Ril, but he was glad to hand over to someone else. He relaxed almost visibly. 'Florrie, where's me slippers? Just got time for supper an' a read o' t'evenin' paper before I go an' meet t'lads at t'Feathers.'

'What's worrying your father?' Ril asked, when she and Norman were outside.

'It's 'ard for you to understand,' said Norman. 'I don't find it all that easy myself. It's sort of built into t'older folk, like, that t'Withenses is t'bosses round 'ere, an' you don't get anywhere by quarrellin' wi' t'boss. And Dad remembers, from 'is dad an' grandad before 'im, that old Caradoc was looked on as a disgrace to t'family, gettin' sent away an' all that. It took years to live 'im down.'

'Miss Withens isn't *my* boss,' said Ril. 'And anyway I'm not quarrelling with her. And why be ashamed of old Caradoc? – I'm proud of him.'

'Miss Withens is a governor of your school,' Norman pointed out. 'And she's Dad's landlord. An' yours as well, if I remember rightly.'

'Do you feel the same as your parents?' Ril asked.

'No,' said Norman. 'I've told you what I feel. You can be proud of Caradoc if you like, but 'e's dead, an' you can't bring 'im to life. If t'old Common ever comes back to t'town it'll be because Miss Withens 'ands it over or because t'town buys it an' pays for it. You're wastin' your time, Ril.'

'However . . .' said Ril.

Norman grinned at her.

'However,' he said, 'you're determined to go through with it.'

'Yes, I am.'

'Well,' said Norman, 'this is what I think you should do. Tell your dad what you've found out so far. Ask 'im if 'e thinks it's enough to be worth takin' any further. An' if it

116

is go to Miss Withens 'erself an' get permission to follow it up. I don't see 'ow anyone can object to that. If my dad says any more about it I'll make 'im see reason.'

'But what if Miss Withens won't give permission?'

'We'll deal with that when it 'appens.'

'All right,' said Ril. 'Agreed. Hullo, what's going on here?'

They were almost at Park Terrace. Hilda came running to meet them. She was wearing her new frock again, and she was full of excitement.

'Come along!' she cried. 'I called to see you, and I gave your father his tea, and I met James Willoughby on the stairs, and Kenneth Ryder came, and his girl-friend, and some friends of theirs, and you know what? – we're having a party. And your father says where are the gramophone records and what about getting some ice, and he says is he too old and square, because if he is he'll take himself to the pictures and leave us to it, but I said heavens no, James is twenty-five if he's a day, so we're not all that young. . . .'

She collapsed breathless against the gatepost.

Ril caught Norman's hand.

'Hurry up!' she said. 'We're having a party!'

She felt gay, and also surprised. It was possible to feel gay in Hallersage.

*

'So,' Ril concluded, 'we know Sir George had a copy of the *Night Thoughts*, and we know it was the sixth book on Shelf 22. And we can be sure Aunt Martha's message means something, because otherwise it would be too big a coincidence for the *Night Thoughts* to be specially marked like that in the inventory.'

There was a thoughtful silence. The party was over. Robert and his daughter, Norman and Hilda sprawled on chairs or rugs, weary because they had all been dancing.

There was a fearsome pile of washing-up which Ril was trying not to think about.

'It would be nice to find the book, wouldn't it?' said Robert. 'If it's still there, of course.'

'The trouble is,' Ril pointed out, 'that it might be anywhere now among all those miles of shelves. It could take days to find.'

'But the message said *behind* the Night Thoughts, not inside it,' said Hilda. 'So most likely it's the position of the book that matters, not the book itself. And we know where the book *was*.'

'The message said *not* behind the Night Thoughts, anyway,' objected Robert. 'So apart from knowing that there's something special about the Night Thoughts we still haven't really got anywhere, have we?'

'It's like 'untin' a black cat on a dark night,' said Norman.

'That "not" is a problem,' admitted Ril.

And at that moment a recollection flashed across her mind: something that might make sense of the message after all.

'I'd like to have another look in that library,' she said. 'I believe I could find something after all.'

'Very well,' said Robert. 'Write to Miss Withens. Tell her the story about your ancestor and how he got friendly with Sir George in his later years, and say that you think some document might be found in Withishall. I don't think you're obliged to tell her what you hope it is, because that's only guesswork.'

'Even so, she may not be keen on the idea,' said Ril.

'You could make it sound like historical research,' suggested Hilda.

'Well, that's what it is, really,' said Robert. 'I can't believe that if you find anything it would have any present-day importance.'

'I think it might,' said Ril doggedly.

'Don't be too disappointed if it doesn't,' said Robert. 'And now I'll get Daisy out and run Hilda home. It's after ten, Hilda. Will your parents be worried?'

'Not they,' said Hilda happily. 'They'll be glad they've been rid of me for a while.'

'I suppose I'd better wash up,' said Ril with a sigh, as her father and Hilda disappeared. 'Golly, what a pile of dishes! Norman, get that cloth and dry for me, there's a pet.'

'My father never dries t'dishes,' said Norman as he prepared to help. 'He says it's woman's work.'

'Well, you keep telling me he's old-fashioned,' said Ril. 'That proves it.'

Norman made no reply. Both he and Ril were too tired for conversation. They stood side by side in a companionable silence, broken only by the occasional chinking of plates and the lapping of dishwater. The stack of dirty dishes dwindled; the stack of clean ones grew.

'There, it wasn't so bad after all, was it?' said Ril, when the job was done.

Norman recalled himself from a daydream of an unusually domestic kind.

'Nicest lot o' dishes I ever dried in my life,' he said.

11

Ril showed the letter to her father before posting it.

Dear Miss Withens, [it ran]

Thank you for a most enjoyable afternoon at Withishall, yesterday. It was of special interest to me to visit the house, because I have a connexion with it which may surprise you. I am a descendant of Caradoc Clough, of whom I expect you have heard.

He was the leader of the peasants' revolt which you mentioned in conversation.

You may know that as an old man Caradoc Clough often visited Sir George Withens at the hall, and I have come across some information which suggests that some interesting documents might be found there. I wonder if you would allow me to spend a morning in your library one day soon, following up an idea which has occurred to me. I promise that I will not be a nuisance and that I will show you anything I find.

Yours sincerely,
Ril Terry

'Yes, that's all right,' said Robert. 'A bit formal perhaps, but I don't suppose that will do any harm. And a bit vague — but maybe that's just as well.' He smiled at his daughter. 'Now we'll have to see what she says.'

'I simply can't wait,' said Ril; but she had to. There was no reply during the next week. Meanwhile the heat-wave broke up in thunderstorms, to be followed by two or three wet and wretched days. Ril caught up with some reading, and wrote a few letters to friends in Belhampton, and went once to the pictures with Hilda.

Perhaps my previous letter didn't reach you (she wrote to Celia a week later). *This is what it said* ... And she put her request again. But still there was no reply.

The weather stayed cold and damp. Ril helped her father to sort out his lecture-notes and timetables. He was busier than ever now, for enrolments were due to begin in three weeks' time. Ril also tried to write some poems, but found she was still out of touch. Her thoughts kept turning to Withishall.

Although I have had no answer, she wrote to Celia after another week, *I still hope you will consider my request....*

But by now the silence was deafening. A few days later Ril plucked up courage and dialled Celia's number.

'Withishall,' said a voice.

'May I speak to Miss Withens, please?'

'What name is it?'

'Ril Terry.'

'Just a moment, please. No, I'm sorry, Miss Withens is not at home. No, I don't know when she'll be in. No, I can't take a message. Good-bye.'

Next day Ril dialled the number again. Miss Withens answered the telephone herself.

'Celia Withens here.'

'Good morning, Miss Withens. This is Ril Terry speaking. I'm sorry to bother you, but . . .'

A click, and the dialling tone followed. Celia had rung off.

    *

'Miss Withens won't even speak to me,' Ril told Norman when he called the next day. 'It's funny, because we seemed to be getting on quite well. She said I must come again – at least I thought she did. Perhaps she meant Roy after all.'

'She must 'a' meant Roy,' said Norman. ''E's been visitin' at Withis'all two or three times. An', what's more, I think she's been out with 'im.'

'She must like him then.'

'Accordin' to Roy it was a slow start but now she thinks 'e's t'cat's whiskers. 'E says she told 'im that most o' t'men she knows are nothin' but layabouts, compared wi' a feller like 'im that's built up 'is own business from scratch. That's what 'e says, anyroad.'

'It could be true,' said Ril thoughtfully. 'I wonder if he'd be right for her.'

Norman stared.

'You mean – gettin' married?'

'Why not? They'd make a lovely couple. And she seems

121

to me to be quite lonely. And wouldn't it be nice if she could settle down here in Hallersage?'

'Nay, lass,' said Norman. 'That's summat you can rule right out. She'd 'ave to be proper daft to wed Roy. You take it from me, 'e's a bad 'un.'

'I don't believe anybody's entirely bad,' said Ril; and then, returning to her theme: 'Anyway, if they're getting on so well you'd think they might be pleased with me for introducing them.'

'You know what?' said Norman. 'I think t'best thing we can do is go round and 'ave a word wi' Roy. At least 'e can't shut 'isself up in a castle an' refuse to speak to you.'

*

The showrooms gleamed with plate-glass and chrome and coloured tiles. 'Quality Cars (Hallersage) Ltd' said the neon sign. Norman and Ril stood in the doorway and watched Roy deal with a customer.

'I can tell you know a good car when you see one, sir,' he was saying. 'Yes, this is a beauty. One owner, low mileage, chauffeur-driven. Completely overhauled since it came to us. And what's more, sir – I wouldn't tell everybody this, but I can see you're asking yourself how we can be selling it so cheaply – the fact is that we're selling it at a loss. Half a dozen new cars coming in tomorrow and we've got to have the space.'

'Could you keep it till this afternoon?' asked the customer.

Roy gestured with both hands.

'At this price, sir? Impossible. I could sell it four or five times over. Of course you can risk it if you like, but I'm afraid you'd be letting it slip through your fingers.'

'Well, yes, I can see it's a very nice car . . .' began the customer.

''E's on the hook all right,' commented Norman. 'Another ten minutes an' 'e'll 'ave signed on t'dotted line.'

The forecast was accurate. Within the quarter-hour Roy had disposed of the customer and the car as well. He rolled his eyes comically.

'Just can't stop selling cars,' he said. 'It's like a disease. I've got it badly. And how are my two young friends this morning?'

Norman went straight to the point.

'Are you still seeing Celia Withens?' he asked baldly.

'Tact, dear boy, tact,' said Roy in the best showroom accent. 'You must learn to approach these matters with greater delicacy.'

'Well, are you?' demanded Norman.

'Yes,' said Roy, 'I am. And may I ask, my dear Norman, what the devil it has to do with you?'

'It's to do with me really,' said Ril. 'I've written her some letters and she hasn't answered.'

'I'm not her secretary,' said Roy.

'But you knew she'd got the letters.'

'Yes,' said Roy. 'Yes, I knew.'

'Roy,' said Ril, 'this is important to me. Could you persuade her to let me do as I asked?'

Roy looked at her quizzically.

'With the best will in the world,' he said, 'I don't think I could.'

'Do you know why she won't let me?'

'You'd better ask her,' said Roy.

Ril turned sharply to see that the red Jaguar was standing outside the showrooms, with Celia at the wheel. She was waving something in her hand.

Roy strode out on to the pavement.

'I got the tickets,' Celia said. Her face was full of animation. She handed him an envelope. 'I'll see you at seven-thirty at the Travellers' Bar. We'll have a drink first. Good-bye till then.'

Ril and Norman were now standing at Roy's side.

'Miss Withens . . .' Ril began.

Celia frowned. For a moment it looked as if she might drive off without a word. Then she seemed to change her mind.

'You want to speak to me?' she said sharply.

'Yes, please.'

'I'll take you to Maggie's for coffee. Both of you. Jump in.'

At a corner table behind a potted palm Celia surveyed her guests. Her manner was much less friendly than at Withishall.

'Well,' she said, 'I suppose it's about this treasure-hunt or whatever it is.'

'Yes.'

'I should have thought your letters had answered themselves by now,' said Celia.

'You mean . . .'

'I mean I'm not having anything to do with that kind of nonsense.'

'But it won't do any harm.'

'Won't it? What are you aiming at? Come on, out with it!'

'Well,' said Ril awkwardly, 'we thought some light might be thrown on Sir George Withens's intentions about the old Common.'

'I see. A matter of purely historical interest?'

'Not entirely,' Ril admitted.

'No indeed. You want to shake my title to some of the Withens land. I've heard a bit of this folklore before, you know. Well, you wouldn't get anywhere. But in any case I'm not going to let you try. If you think I'll let a silly schoolgirl come digging around in my library you're mistaken.'

Ril bit her lip. She felt tears coming to her eyes.

Celia lit a cigarette. Then she looked into Ril's face and softened a little.

'You know what?' she said. 'I rather liked you at first, Ril. I felt there was some sympathy between us. I didn't care for it a bit when I got your letter and realized that you were after something, just like all the rest.'

Ril was hurt, and said nothing. But Norman, who had previously been silent, leaned across the table.

'That's t'real point, isn't it?' he said. 'You're afraid of somebody takin' advantage. I don't believe you care tuppence for old Sir George, or for t'Withens land either.'

'Norman, don't be so rude!' said Ril, horrified.

But Norman was on the offensive now.

'I'll tell you summat more, Miss Withens. You're on t'road to bein' made a fool of, all right. But not by us!'

Ril feared an outburst. But when Celia spoke it was with cold dignity.

'Thank you for your company,' she said, 'and for the demonstration of manners. Pay the bill out of this, will you? Good-bye.'

*

'I don't care what you say,' said Ril. 'I still feel sorry for her, and in a way I still like her.'

'You've no cause to. She's as 'ard as nails.'

'I'm not so sure. I think she's the kind of person who gets hurt.'

'Anyroad, you 'aven't got any change out of 'er, 'ave you?'

'I haven't,' Ril admitted.

'What are you going to do, then?'

'It looks like the end of the road, doesn't it?'

'You're not goin' to take it lying down!' Norman asserted.

'I haven't any choice.'

'Now look 'ere. 'Ow long do you think it'll take you to find whatever it is, once you're in t'library?'

'If what I think is correct, only a few minutes. But if I can't get into Withishall I can't do a thing.'

'Who says you can't get into Withis'all?'

Ril was startled.

'What do you mean?'

'I reckon we could both get in quite easy,' said Norman.

After a moment's stunned silence Ril said:

'You mean we should break in?'

Norman nodded.

'Oh, don't be silly, Norman. It would – why, it would be burglary!'

'Listen,' said Norman. 'This thing you're lookin' for belongs to t'Cloughs, doesn't it? Well, we're t'Cloughs. There's nowt wrong wi' lookin' for summat of your own, is there?'

'I don't think Celia would see it like that,' said Ril doubtfully. 'Anyway, Norman, I thought you weren't interested. Why the sudden enthusiasm?'

Norman was shamefaced.

'Well, to tell you t'truth I've got more interested as it went on,' he admitted. 'Not that I really think you'll find owt, even now. But it's worth 'avin' a try.'

'Norman, we can't.'

''Course we can. Let's go tonight.'

Ril felt butterflies in her stomach.

'Tonight!' she echoed. 'That's sudden, isn't it?'

'Sooner t'better,' said Norman. 'Let's do it while t'weather's fine. It's a long way up to t'house. It wouldn't be much fun in t'rain. An' there won't be much moon tonight – that's just as well.'

'But how will we get in?'

'I'd like to see t'door or window that'll stop me.'

'You sound like a professional,' said Ril.

'Well, I'm not one. But I'll make a proper job of it. Do you know where t'library is?'

'Yes, it's on the first floor, at the corner with the wing.'

'We'll get in all right,' said Norman. 'I'll take a few tools. And a coil o' rope. I've got fifty or sixty foot of 'alf-inch rope that'd take a person's weight if necessary.'

'I haven't said I'm coming.'

'Well, you are,' said Norman. 'Now listen, I'll call for you at 'alf past twelve. You'd better wear slacks an' a sweater an' plimsolls. An' bring a torch with you, because we'll need one each. . . .'

Ril had never seen him so eager. She remembered Florrie's words: "'E's got plenty o' spirit, 'as t'lad, and 'e's adventurous, like.'

Too adventurous by half, thought Ril.

12

It was ten minutes past one. The last light had just gone out in Withishall. The night was mild, with a light wind. Norman and Ril crouched behind a great urn at the entrance to the ornamental gardens. Five yards away stood the urn's twin; in front of them were thirty yards of gravel, then the façade of the house.

They had picked out the library some time ago. Directly below it was a great bay window that had been added in the last century to the drawing-room. It was a blister on the classical front of the house, thought Ril, but a blessing to burglars. A few feet away from it was a fall-pipe.

'Piece o' cake,' whispered Norman. 'We'll give 'em another ten minutes, then I'll go up that pipe. I can jump across to t'top o' t'bay and open t'library window. When I'm ready I'll wave, an' you can nip over. I'll get you up there some'ow.'

'How will we get down again?'

'We'll let ourselves down wi' t'rope. Sling it round summat.'

The butterflies fluttered in Ril's stomach. She did not like the programme at all.

'Norman, I'm frightened,' she said. 'Let's go home.'

Norman squeezed her hand.

'You're all right, lass,' he said. 'I won't let owt 'appen to you. Up the Cloughs!'

'Up the Cloughs!' Ril echoed wanly. And a moment later Norman had risen from her side and was racing soundlessly across the gravel towards the house.

There she lost sight of him. From where she was only the upper part of the fall-pipe could be seen; the lower part was hidden in shadow. Minutes passed. Ril wondered whether Norman had failed to get off the ground. Then she saw a confused movement as though the fall-pipe itself was wriggling. As she strained her eyes, the sight resolved itself into Norman, several feet up and climbing well. And a moment later there was a sudden silent movement like the flitting of a shadow, as he leaped from the pipe to the top of the bay.

Ril could now see the back of his head and shoulders as he busied himself with one of the library windows. For agonizing minutes he stood there, while she wiped her damp palms on her handkerchief and the butterflies fluttered again and again. Ridiculously, she expected lights to flash on all over the house at any moment. And then Norman had stepped to the edge of the bay and was waving his arms in wide sweeps.

Ril got up. Her legs were like water. It seemed more by will power than muscle that she propelled herself across the gravel to the side of the house. But she found the fall-pipe and felt its metal cold against her hands.

She had forgotten how to climb. She had forgotten everything. For a minute she just stood. Then she looked up and saw Norman gesturing from the top of the bay. A fragment of self-possession came back. If he could do it, she could. Scrabbling and slithering, going two feet up and one back, she worked her way up the pipe. Once she slipped, and lost four or five feet. But eventually she was on a level with Norman, and had her feet on a bracket that held the fall-pipe to the wall.

There was now a jump of about four feet from the fall-pipe to the top of the bay. How Norman had managed it Ril did not know, for the bracket was a poor take-off point and it would be impossible to get any impetus for the leap. She clung to the pipe for two or three minutes, panting. Then she took a deep breath and hurled herself across.

With one toe she felt the flat top of the bay beneath her. The other foot was in mid-air. Momentarily she swayed back and thought she was going to fall. Then Norman gripped her. Miraculously she was standing safely on both feet, and in front of her was the open window. She climbed through it and sank in a heap on the library floor.

'Are you all right?' hissed Norman.

'I'm fine,' said Ril weakly. 'Just let me pull myself together.'

She was suffering slightly from shock. But Norman stood beside her making impatient cluckings. She dragged herself to her feet.

'We'll draw t'curtains,' whispered Norman, 'then we can use our torches.'

Quietly they drew the curtains across the library's four windows. Ril had a glimpse of the new moon. The wind was rising a little.

She moved towards the library door and the shelf where once the Night Thoughts had stood. And almost at once she bumped into something. She clutched it with both hands. Norman shone a light and Ril found herself looking into the eyes of one of the bronze figures. She started back.

'You brought a torch, didn't you?' said Norman roughly. 'Use it.'

Ril felt for the torch in the pocket of her slacks, and shone it up towards the shelf she wanted.

'Can you see the library steps?' she asked softly.

Norman flashed his light round.

'They're over here,' he said. Cautiously he pushed the steps across. Ril climbed to the top and could reach the highest shelf comfortably. She was relieved to find that the glass doors were still not locked.

She eased two or three books out and handed them down to Norman; then a few more, until she had cleared the first eighteen inches or so of the shelf. Then she shone the torch into the gap she had made.

There was nothing to be seen but the wooden panelling behind. But her recollection was correct. The wood was not perfect. Varnish did not quite conceal a small round blemish.

'I've found it!' she whispered. 'The knot!'

'The what?'

'The knot!' Ril repeated in growing ecstasy. 'The knot! The knot behind the *Night Thoughts*!'

*

Ril pressed on the knot with her forefinger, gently at first and then harder. It was something of an anticlimax. No doors slid smoothly back, no Aladdin's cave stood revealed. She thought at first that nothing had happened. But shining the torch into the gap again she saw that the panel had shifted slightly and there was now a narrow crack along the edge.

She tried to get her fingers into the crack, but it was not wide enough.

'Got a penknife?' she whispered to Norman.

'Of course I 'ave.'

'Pass it up to me.'

130

'No, get down an' let me 'ave a go.'

'I said pass it up to me!'

'Oh, all right!'

Norman handed over a stout penknife. Ril nearly split her thumbnail opening it. Then she inserted the biggest blade into the crack and levered gently. The edge of the panel moved forward half an inch. She got her fingers to it and tugged. At first it resisted. Then she almost toppled backwards as it came away. She handed the panel to Norman. Where it had been there was now a dirty, crumble-edged gap in the plaster, a mere half-inch deep, and just wide enough to hold what it did hold – a foolscap envelope, discoloured and covered with dust.

Ril seized it, blew on it, wiped it on her sleeve, and shone the torch on to it from close range. The ink of the address had yellowed almost to vanishing-point. But she could still read it. In a clear though wavery hand it said: *To Mr Caradoc Clough.*

'Got it!' she hissed in triumph. 'Got it!' And, forgetting in her elation where she was, she stepped back, trod on air, and fell. With blind instinct she grabbed with her free hand for something to save herself, but caught only some books in the shelf she had been clearing. As she fell on top of Norman the books clattered to the floor. At the same moment the steps overbalanced and crashed into the glass of a lower shelf. Ril got up, dashed in panic towards the window, and bumped into one of the bronzes. Over it went, plinth and all. In the silent house the noise was deafening.

Ril got to the window and flung it up. Norman was beside her.

'Don't jump!' he cried. 'You'll break your neck!'

'Let the rope down, then.'

Now that disaster had struck, Ril felt her presence of mind returning.

Norman shone his torch about him.

'I can't see owt to sling t'rope round,' he said.

A fresh thought occurred to Ril.

'Quick!' she said. 'Down through the house and we'll let ourselves out!'

It was worth trying. Still holding the envelope, she ran for the library door and out into the corridor. Everything was still in darkness. Was it possible that nobody had heard the noise? Ril knew that the servants' quarters were some distance away at the back of the house. But Celia . . . ?

Ril picked her way rapidly along the corridor. In a few seconds she had reached the head of the branching main staircase. She ran lightly down and crossed the hall to the front door. There was still no sound. It looked as though they would get safely away. And then, as Ril shone her light, looking for the latch, she heard the sounds of an approaching car outside, and the crunch of wheels on gravel as it braked.

She darted back towards the staircase, but was only half-way up when the door opened, lights flashed on, and Celia Withens stepped into the hall. It had not occurred to either Ril or Norman that Celia might still be out.

Ril crouched motionless on the stairs, in the forlorn hope of not being noticed. But Celia saw her at once. Her look of astonishment was followed by one of fury. And in a moment her eye fell on the envelope which Ril was clutching instinctively to her chest.

'What have you got there?' she called. 'Come down and give it to me!'

Ril said nothing and retreated. Celia ran towards the steps. And as she chased Ril up one branch of the staircase Norman emerged at top speed from the corridor and hurtled down the other, two or three steps at a time.

'Chuck it down, Ril!' he called.

With a flicking movement, Ril sent the envelope flying down. It floated sideways for several feet. Norman turned to pursue it. Celia ran back down the stairs towards him. Ril followed her, meaning to make a dash for the outer door if she got a chance. But as she did so the door opened again and Roy appeared. This was something else that she and Norman had not thought of; obviously Roy had been escorting Celia home after an evening out.

Ril ran back up one staircase and Norman, who now had the envelope, ran up the other.

'This way!' Ril shouted, for she had thought of a last chance of escape. Back past the library door she sped, and round the corner into the wing. Another corridor stretched ahead of her, and at the end of it was the door into the bell-tower.

Norman was some distance behind, having had to run round the landing from the stair-head. And behind Norman was Roy. From below Ril heard Celia shout:

'Get that envelope, Roy!'

Ril was still well ahead when she reached the door to the bell-tower. She opened it, stepped inside, and held it open for Norman.

With the rope over one arm and the envelope in his hand, Norman was handicapped. Roy was gaining on him – but not quite rapidly enough. Norman raced through the door. Ril flung it to, and shot the bolt a split second before Roy's weight thudded against the door.

The door shook slightly but held. It was stout. Ril saw that there was a second bolt at the top, and shot that one as well.

A moment later there was another thud as Roy put his shoulder to the door. Again it shuddered and again it held.

'Down to the bottom!' cried Ril. 'There must be a way out!'

Round and round, down and down the spiral staircase they ran. There was a door at the bottom. But it must have been unused for years. Cobwebs covered it. Norman tugged at the bolt with his fingers, failed to move it, kicked it, and kicked it again. This time it shifted, and a third kick knocked it right back. Hopefully they tugged at the door. But it was locked as well as bolted. The light of their torches showed no key and no likely hiding-place. Meanwhile two more thuds and an ominous creak came from the door above, which Roy was still battering.

'There's only one hope,' Ril said. 'Up to the top and down by the rope!'

Up they ran again. They passed the door by which they had entered the tower. By now the sounds had ceased. It looked as though Roy had given up for the moment. Up and up they went until, breathless, they reached the bare round room that had been Sir George Withens's study. Here there was another door with a bolt, and they fastened it behind them. That made two barriers between pursued and pursuers.

Ril had hoped it would be possible to fasten the rope to something in this room and climb out through a window. She had forgotten that the windows were narrow and imitation-medieval. Nothing much bigger than a cat could have got through.

'Up again!' she cried. And they went up the iron ladder and pushed open the trapdoor at the top. A fresh breeze blew in their faces. They were in the open air, on the gallery surrounding the bell-frame. Clouds scudded across the sky, and beyond the tree-tops of the park they could see, far down the valley, the lights of Hallersage.

Norman looked over the railing.

'I doubt if t'rope's long enough,' he said. 'An' it's a dangerous climb. You can't do it, Ril.'

'What do we do, then?' Ril demanded. 'Give up? Not on your life!'

She had been nervous about the whole enterprise, but now her blood was up. She was not going to humiliate herself by surrendering to Roy and Celia and handing over Caradoc's letter.

'We'll make it yet!' she declared. 'Let's tie our rope to the end of the bell-rope – that'll give us a few extra feet.'

'Is t'bell-rope sound? We don't want to break our necks.'

'Should be all right,' said Ril. 'Fasten it to the frame, so we don't ring the bell.'

They pulled the bell-rope up from the ringing-chamber below. Norman knotted it tightly round the frame just below the wheel, so that any weight on the rope would be taken by the frame and not by the bell. He inspected the bell-rope rapidly by torchlight and seemed satisfied. Then he tied his own rope to the end of it and threw the coil over the railing.

'It might just about reach,' he said. 'Can't be far short, anyway. I'll go first. Don't start till I call you – t'rope might not bear both of us at once.'

Before Ril could say anything he was over the railing and on his way down.

There was still no sound from inside the tower. She looked over the edge and saw Norman was descending rapidly but unevenly, sometimes going hand over fist, other times sliding for several feet at a stretch. The rope swayed in the wind, and several times he bumped against the wall of the tower. Eventually she lost sight of him in the shadows. But a minute later he called out:

'All right! Come on now, Ril. T'rope's long enough. I'll hold t'end for you.'

Ril had no time to be frightened. Over she went. She knew how to climb a rope, but this wasn't like a gymnasium exercise. Still, it was easier for her than it had been for Norman, because he was keeping the rope steady. She let herself slide for a few feet, but tore her hands and only just managed to brake with her feet. That shook her and she went on more cautiously. It seemed miles to the ground.

Then suddenly the rope lost its bottom anchor and Ril swung against the wall with a thud that knocked the breath out of her. She looked down. There was only about twenty feet to go now, but she saw that two figures were struggling below: Norman and Roy. Of course! Roy had given up the pursuit inside the tower and had run round outside.

Ril put on speed but was not fast enough. Roy seized the rope, Norman grabbed Roy, and for a few seconds the rope was bearing the weight of all three.

It held. But from up above came a strange, cracking sound. Then the bell chimed once, not at full tilt but with a hollow, ominous boom. There were more cracking noises and a fearful metallic jarring. In a flash Ril realized what had happened. The rope had held but the bell frame had given way.

She jumped for her life.

'Run!' she shouted. 'Run!'

Norman and Roy had about half a second.

It was just enough.

There was a rush of wind, a momentary impression of something hurtling through the air, and a thud that shook the ground. The bell that had stood guard over the Withens estate for a hundred and thirty years had crashed to earth. All three of them had missed being killed by inches.

They stood immobile for some seconds. The recent pursuit seemed dwarfed by the fall of the bell. Then Norman took to his heels and vanished in the darkness among the ornamental gardens. Immediately Roy was after him. Ril stood by herself, her legs too weak to let her move.

But now there were voices, male and female. Lights came on in several windows. A great lamp lit up the portico. Feet crunched the gravel, and Ril heard Celia call some incomprehensible instruction. Strength came back to her and she fled.

*

Ril raced across the lawns of the ornamental gardens,

leaped over flower-beds, and pushed her way through hedges until she was in the open parkland. Here the grass was damp and fairly long, and the going was hard. She ran from tree to tree, looking round at intervals. There was no sign of Roy or Norman; no indication that anybody was chasing her; no sound except her own pounding heart. Taking her bearings from the lights of the house she ran and ran. After some minutes she saw the headlamps of a car travelling down the drive away from the house; otherwise there was nothing to tell her what was happening.

She was held up at the river-bank and ran along it for many yards until she came to a place where the water was broad and shallow. She plunged through it, getting wet to her knees. Soon afterwards she tripped over something and fell flat, knocking all the breath out of her body; but she got up and floundered on.

Time became meaningless. This nightmare scramble had lasted all her life and was going to last for ever. She was among the trees now, and had lost her sense of direction, but still she stumbled along unseeing. She almost ran into the wall of the estate. And she would not have known at what point she had reached it if she had not immediately seen, only a few yards away, the tree that stretched over the wall.

Her torn hands were hurting now, and it was torture to climb the tree, but by sheer willpower she forced herself along the overhanging branch. She dropped down outside the wall, and sank into a heap on the grass verge of the road. Now that she was outside Withishall she could not have moved another yard.

It might have been five minutes later or it might have been half an hour when Ril heard scrabbling sounds along the branch above. With an effort she raised her head to look. It was Norman.

'Hullo,' she whispered feebly.

''Ullo.'

'Where's Roy?'

''Ome and in bed by now, I should think. 'E soon gave up. After I lost 'im I saw lights goin' down t'drive, an' you can bet your boots it was Roy gettin' away from t'scene.'

'Have you got the envelope?'

'Oh aye,' said Norman grimly, 'an' a fine price we look like payin' for it.' He drew it from under his jersey. 'After all this it better 'adn't be empty.'

Ril took the letter and turned it over. There was light enough to see that it was sealed with an unbroken wax seal. It didn't feel empty.

'Let's hope it's something worth while,' she said.

'We'll take it straight to my father,' she continued. 'I'll wake him up. And we'd better hurry because if we're not quick someone might be there before us.'

She felt better now, and it was downhill all the way. They trotted along the verge of the road, ready to lose themselves if any vehicle came past. But nothing came. Across the market-place they went, down the Old Hallersage Road, and into Park Terrace.

In a window of the floor above the Terrys' flat a light was still shining.

'It'll be James!' said Ril. 'He often works late.' And she remembered that James Willoughby was a lawyer. 'Let's take the envelope to him!'

*

Ril tapped at the door. After a moment James appeared – blue-chinned, tousle-haired, and dressing-gowned. He stared at their torn clothes and dirty faces.

'You'd better come in,' he said. 'I thought for a moment I'd dreamed you. A fine sight you are in the grey dawn after a night of slogging over law books. Now tell me what it's all about. Why are you up at this time?'

'Well, you see . . .' Ril began, but James interrupted.

'Ril, your hands !' he exclaimed. 'Let me look !'

Ril held them up. They were not a pretty sight : smeared with dried blood and dirt, and with two or three fingernails broken.

'Goodness,' she said, 'it's like Lady Macbeth.'

'I hope not that,' said James austerely. 'Come and wash them, and we'll put some disinfectant on.'

'Well, if somebody comes asking whether I've been climbing down a rope I'll hardly be able to deny it,' said Ril.

She and Norman washed their hands and faces, and dabbed disinfectant on their sores. Norman had put the envelope on James's table, and James cast several curious glances at it.

Ril told him, briefly, the story of the night's escapade As she did so, his face lengthened.

'I'm surprised at you,' he said when she paused for breath. 'I'd have thought you had more sense.'

His tone was chilly. Ril glanced at him apprehensively but went on to the end.

'And so,' she concluded, 'this is the envelope Sir George left for Caradoc Clough, and seeing you're a lawyer I want you to open it.'

'Seeing I'm a lawyer,' said James, 'I certainly won't.'

Ril decided not to argue. She seized the envelope, ripped it open, and pulled out the contents. James opened his mouth to protest, but was too late.

'There !' she said. 'All my own work. Now, James, legal etiquette doesn't prevent you from just listening, does it? I'll read it out – if I can read it at all, that is.' For the ink was yellow, and the handwriting thin and shaky. There were two sheets. Ril read from the first :

Withishall, Yorks, June 4th 1867.

Dear Mr Clough,

I am little disposed in this my eighty-fifth year to enter upon the arguments that would ensue were I to make any change in my testamentary dispositions. No doubt however you will know how to make use of the enclosed document.

Y^{rs} sinc^{rly} , Geo. Withens

Ril turned over and read from the second sheet.

To whom it may concern –

I, George Withens, of Withishall in the West Riding of York-shire, baronet, do hereby declare that notwithstanding any provision to the contrary that may appear in my will I do give, devise and bequeath all that land allotted to me in 1825 on the enclosure of Old Hallersage Common, to the Mayor, Aldermen and citizens of the town of Hallersage, to have and to hold upon trust for the benefit of the said town for ever.

Given under my hand this fourth day of June, 1867, George Withens.

Ril slapped the papers down on the table. Joy welled up in her. She kissed Norman, she kissed James.

'We've won!' she cried elatedly. 'We've won! I don't care if I go to jail for this. We've won!'

Then she saw that her elation was not shared by the other two.

Ril looked anxiously from one to the other.

''Ave we won, James?' inquired Norman.

James shook his head.

'I suppose that document isn't witnessed, Ril?' he asked.

'No.'

'Well, it makes no difference – it wouldn't stand up any-way. No court would look at it. I'm sorry to tell you that if it ever had any legal validity it certainly hasn't any today. The Common belongs to the Withenses as much as ever it did.'

'You mean,' said Ril incredulously, 'you mean we've burgled Withishall, risked our necks, brought the bell down, and probably got ourselves into every kind of trouble, and all for nothing?'

James nodded.

'I'm afraid so,' he said.

After the excitement of the quest Ril could barely grasp the immensity of the disappointment. Her first reaction was one of pointless fury.

'Damn Withishall!' she cried. 'Oh damn, damn, damn!'

'Cheer up, love,' said Norman. 'At least t'story's finished. We know what t'old squire intended, even if nowt'll ever come of it. I thought you were interested in history – well, now you can say you've wrote a chapter yourself.'

Ril was silent now. Slowly, tears began to roll down her cheeks.

'Ril, you're all in,' said James. 'Now I'll tell you what we'll do. You go straight to bed. I'll give you a couple of tablets to make you sleep. Leave those papers with me. At breakfast-time I'll take them down to your father and tell him everything that happened. I shall advise him to put them in his own solicitors' hands the moment the office opens. They'll probably get in touch with Cassells, who act for Withishall. There's a chance that Miss Withens hasn't called the police – I can see good reasons why she shouldn't. With a bit of luck we'll get matters straightened out and no one will be any the worse.'

'Or any better,' Ril said ruefully.

'You know what, James? I've 'ad an idea,' said Norman. ''Op it, Ril – you can stay in t'dark for once. Go on, off you go. Now, James, this is it . . .'

Ril walked, very slowly, to the door. Norman was speaking in a low voice to James. As she let herself out of the flat she heard James's comment:

'Good heavens, no! You'll have me struck off the rolls!'

But his tone of voice sounded to Ril like that of a man who might be persuaded.

13

Tiredness, and the tablets James had given her, did their work on Ril. She was just conscious enough to undress and crawl into bed before falling into a bottomless well of sleep. Hours later she floated to the surface, to find a tray with a bowl of soup in front of her, Robert on a chair at the bedside, and Hilda Woodward sitting on the bed.

Ril looked at her father apprehensively. It was not often that she felt his disapproval, and when she did she found it hard to bear. But Robert did not seem as angry as he might have been.

'What you did was very wrong,' he said. 'You must never do such a thing again. You understand?'

'Yes, Daddy.'

'Promise?'

'Yes. Goodness, I never *could* do it again, as long as I live.'

'All right. We'll leave it at that.'

'Where are the documents?' asked Ril.

'I took them in to our lawyer, Mr Linton, as James suggested. And Mr Linton telephoned Cassell and Sons, who act for the Withishall Estate. And they told him they'd have to inform old Mr Cassell himself, who was up at Withishall that very moment. . . .'

Ril pulled a face.

'And later Mr Cassell rang back and asked for the documents to be sent round by special messenger. He wouldn't tell Mr Linton what they intended to do. So we just have to await developments. But I feel fairly hopeful, because if there was going to be serious trouble I think we'd have had the police round before now.'

'I think Ril's wonderful,' said Hilda.

'I think she's a menace,' said Robert. He tried unsuccessfully to look fierce.

Ril took a mouthful of soup. It tasted good, and she was hungry.

'You're letting me off too lightly,' she said. 'I'd feel better if you could play the heavy parent for once. Beat me or put me on bread-and-water for a week – that's what I deserve.'

But playing the heavy parent was not in Robert's line. He could only squeeze his daughter's hand and ask her how she felt.

'I feel fine,' said Ril, 'and I'm going to get up in a minute.' She ate some more soup.

'I suppose it's all my own fault,' said Robert. 'I hadn't realized you were getting obsessed by the Withishall business. I've been so tied up with planning my courses that I haven't been much company for you.'

'You see?' said Ril to Hilda. 'He's just too understanding to be true.'

While she dressed, Hilda made a late lunch. It was half past two by the time they finished the meal.

Hilda was still full of admiration.

'I'd never have dared to do what you did!' she said. 'And to think the papers were still there after all those years. It brings history to life, doesn't it?'

'It doesn't bring the Common back to Hallersage,' said Ril.

Then the telephone rang.

Ril jumped. She had not realized she was so nervous. Her hand shook as she picked the receiver up.

'Hilltop 2499,' she said.

'Can I speak to Miss Terry?' asked a feminine voice.

'Speaking.'

'Just hold on a minute, please,' said the voice: and then, to someone else: 'Your call to Miss Terry.'

An interval.

'Is that Miss Terry?' asked a second voice.

'Speaking,' said Ril again.

'Hold the line, Miss Terry.'

Another interval. Ril began to get restless. Then a third voice, smooth and masculine.

'Miss Terry?'

'Speaking.'

'Please hold on for a call from Mr Samuel Thwaite.'

And in the background she heard the words, 'Miss Terry is on the line now, sir.'

Finally came the voice of Sam Thwaite himself – fresh, gusty, and a little too loud.

'Are you t'young lady I gave a lift into town from t'school a few weeks back?'

'Yes,' said Ril.

'You was up to some mischief at Withis'all last night, wasn't you?'

'Well . . .' began Ril cautiously.

'Well nothin'. I'm sendin' t'car round. I want to see you right away.'

And Sam Thwaite rang off.

*

Robert wanted to go with his daughter, but she persuaded him to stay behind in case Mr Linton telephoned again. In a few minutes' time Sam Thwaite's wizened little chauffeur was at the door. In the street stood the splendid elderly Rolls.

Two or three children had gathered round. Ril swept past them and let the chauffeur open the door. After all, it wasn't every day that you had a Rolls-Royce calling for you.

The Rolls sailed majestically down the main road into Hallersage and pulled up at the door of an impressive gilt-

and-gingerbread building with marble walls and mosaic floor. In engraved gold lettering over the entrance were the words 'Thwaite House'.

'She's come to see Sam,' said the chauffeur to the commissionaire.

'Oh aye,' said the commissionaire. 'Sam'll see 'er. 'Op into t'lift, lass. First floor.

On the first floor a secretary sat at a reception desk. She looked at Ril inquiringly.

'Miss Terry, to see Mr Thwaite,' Ril said.

'Oh yes, Miss Terry. Mr Thwaite will see you. Follow me, please.'

She led the way to a little waiting-room, where a second secretary took over.

'Just sit down, Miss Terry. Mr Thwaite is expecting you.'

Ril sat down. A minute later a young man in a charcoal-grey suit emerged from an inner door and spoke in the polished tone Ril had heard on the telephone:

'Will you come this way, please, Miss Terry?'

Ril followed him into a big, high, old-fashioned room, treading gingerly across a venerable Turkey-red carpet. In a corner was an enormous mahogany desk, with heavy, glass inkstand, leather-edged blotter, and carved cigar-box. Up from behind it rose the impressive bulk of Mr Samuel Thwaite.

He beamed.

'Well, lass!' he said. 'So you did it! Clear out, Billy, I want to talk to t'lass in private. Well, lass, so you busted into Withis'all! Eh, I'd 'a' liked to see yon Celia Withens's face!'

'How did you know?' asked Ril, staring.

'Aha!' said Sam. 'Listen to this 'ere. "*To whom it may concern. I, George Withens, of Withis'all in t'West Ridin' o' Yorkshire, baronet . . .*"'

'But,' gasped Ril, 'I thought the documents had gone back to Withishall!'

'So they 'ave, love, so they 'ave,' Sam Thwaite roared with delight. 'Take a look at this!'

He thrust the paper he had been reading into her hand. It was a photographic copy of Sir George's letter.

'That's your cousin at work,' said Sam happily. 'Fred Clough's lad. 'E's got 'is 'ead screwed on all right, 'as that lad. 'E photographed them papers before they went back. 'E knew I'd be interested. I allus thowt there was summat like this in existence, but I never thowt I'd clap eyes on it!'

'But it's of no legal validity!' said Ril.

''Appen not,' said Sam. ''Appen not. But we'll 'ave fun wi' it. By gum we'll 'ave fun wi' it! An' more than fun! 'Ere, let me look at you, lass. Aye, I'd 'a' known you was a Clough. Cloughs an' Thwaites goes right back to t'old times in 'Allersage, Cloughs an' Thwaites together. My own great-grandad marched wi' Caradoc Clough. We'll make 'er lady-ship, jump, we will an' all!'

'I've nothing against Miss Withens,' said Ril, 'except that she seemed to turn against me and wouldn't let me look for the document. But perhaps she can't be blamed for that, considering what it says.'

'I've nowt agin 'er myself,' said Sam, 'but t'Withenses 'ave bit sittin' on this land that they've no proper right to, when t'Corporation needs it for playin'-fields an' a public park. And that there Celia wouldn't give a ha'porth of it away, any more than t'rest of 'em. An' now she'll 'ave to think again. Eh, lass, I could 'ug you. No legal validity indeed! Old Tom Cassell knows there's more to it than legal validities! I'm goin' to ring 'im now.'

Still beaming, he went to the telephone.

''Ave you seen t'*Chronicle*, lass?' he asked, as he picked up the receiver. And he pushed a copy across the desk.

The *Chronicle* was Hallersage's evening paper. The early edition was out already. And on the front page was a story under heavy headlines:

'The 130-year-old Withishall Bell crashed from its tower to the gravel drive of the hall during high winds last night. Structural weakness in the bell's supporting frame is blamed for the accident.

'The entire Withishall household was abed when the bell crashed down. Servants, sleeping at the rear of the house, rushed out on hearing the noise to find that the Lady of the Manor, Miss Celia Withens, had reached the scene before them.

' "I was staggered to find the bell and part of the frame lying in the drive," said Miss Withens today. "No one had any idea that the bell was unsafe. It is a mercy that the accident happened at night when there was no one around."

'Miss Withens, who has a villa in the South of France and is only temporarily in residence, said that the bell had been cracked by its fall and would not be replaced.

'At first it was thought that someone might have broken into the house. Some glass had been smashed in the library and a bronze figure overturned. But Miss Withens explained that she herself tripped and fell while in the library about bedtime. The accident to the bell was in no way connected with this occurrence.

'The bell was erected in the first half of the last century by Sir George Withens, the fourth baronet . . .'

Ril read no more.

'Well!' she said, astonished. 'So they're passing it off as an accident! I wonder why?'

But Sam Thwaite motioned her to silence. He had got through to Mr Cassell.

''Ullo, Tom,' he was saying. 'Long time sin' I saw you. 'Ow are you? Good. Yes, I'm fine. I see there's been a bit of an accident up at Withis'all. Aye, it's in t'*Chronicle*. But I reckon if t'*Chronicle* knew all that 'ad 'appened it'd make a much better story, eh? You don't know what I'm talkin' about? Come now, Tom lad, yon bonny client o' yours must 'ave told you *summat.* . . .'

Sam gave Ril an enormous wink.

'Now listen, Tom,' he went on, 'I'm goin' to read to you from a little bit o' paper what I'm 'oldin' in my 'and.' And he read out, as he had done to Ril a few minutes earlier:
' "*To whom it may concern. I, George Withens, of Withis'all in t'West Ridin' of Yorkshire* . . ." '

Then he took the receiver quickly from his ear and held it at arm's length. Even Ril could hear the explosive sounds that were coming from it. Sam winked again.

'Eh, Tom, Tom,' he said sorrowfully as soon as there was a pause. 'I'd never 'ave thought you knew all them vulgar words. Now listen, Tom, if t'national Press was to get 'old o' this bit o' paper it'd make no end of a splash. An' it wouldn't put your little Celia in too 'appy a light, would it? Might seem to some folks as if she was tryin' to 'ang on to what wasn't rightly 'ers.

'What's that, Tom? Burglary? Nay, Tom, there 'asn't been no burglary. Miss Withens says so 'erself. She'd 'ave a job to change 'er mind now, wouldn't she? An' even if she did say it was burglary public sympathy might not be on 'er side, you know. Besides, it might come out that there was a young feller in t'motor trade visitin' 'er at one o'clock in t'mornin'. Oh aye, I know 'e was only seein' 'er 'ome, but some folks 'ave nasty suspicious minds.

'Blackmail, you said? 'Ard words, Tom, 'ard words. You're not yourself today, are you? You're shockin' me.' Sam rolled his eyes comically. 'You wouldn't find Sam Thwaite mixed up in blackmail. But, Tom, you remember that a couple o' years ago t'Corporation asked for a meetin' wi' you an' Miss Withens to see if we could come to terms for t'purchase of t'old Common? An' you remember you said your client wasn't interested? Well, I wonder if she might 'ave changed 'er mind since then.

'No, Tom, no connection wi' last night at all. I'm not threatenin' owt. It was just a thought that 'appened to strike me, like. Aye, that's right, Tom, you go an' put it to 'er again. I know t'Corporation's still interested. I don't know who they'd appoint to negotiate, but it might be Alderman Thwaite, seein' 'e knows a bit about property.

'That's it, Tom, that's it. All right, no bones broken. Aye, we must 'ave a drink together one o' these days. Well, I'll be seein' you, Tom. Might be seein' quite a bit of you, eh, if Miss Withens and t'Corporation come to terms? Oh, come off it, Tom, you know they will. So long, Tom.'

Sam replaced the receiver, leaned back, and laughed long and loudly.

'Eh, I enjoyed that!' he said. 'T'biggest shock Tom Cassell's 'ad in all 'is professional career, I'll be bound. And that's nowt compared wi' t'shock your pal Celia's goin' to get when 'e tells 'er about it.'

Ril was worried. 'I don't want to cause any more trouble,' she said.

'That's all right, lass,' said Sam reassuringly. 'You've done your whack. Now leave it to me. You won't 'ear any more about it – except that one o' these days you'll read in t'Chronicle that 'Allersage Corporation an' Miss Celia Withens 'ave agreed on a price for t'transfer o' t'old Common. An' next year, or 'appen t' year after, lads an' lasses from 'Allersage Grammar School will stop travellin' five miles on t'tram on sports days, an' just go round t'corner instead. An' it'll all be thanks to you.'

'I won't be able to tell anyone, though, will I?' asked Ril.

In her daydreams about the recovery of the old Common she had sometimes imagined herself publicly honoured and moving in a blaze of glory.

'No, lass,' said Sam thoughtfully. 'No, you'll 'ave to keep it under your 'at. But it's fair enough, isn't it? If you go breakin' t'law you can't expect to 'ave t'band turn out for you, can you? In fact' – and now Sam looked suddenly fierce – 'you're lucky not to be appearin' in t'Juvenile Court!'

Ril stepped back a pace. Sam roared with laughter again.

'All right, love, all right!' he said. 'Don't worry. But remember: apart from them that know about it already you mustn't tell a soul. An' now if ever you want owt right badly you come an' see Sam Thwaite an' you'll get it, as sure as you're talkin' to t'future Lord 'Allersage. Billy! Show t'young lady out, will you?'

The smooth young man reappeared and led Ril across the thick carpet and through the first door.

'Show Miss Terry out, will you?' he said to the secretary.

'Come this way please, Miss Terry,' said the secretary, and took her as far as the receptionist.

'Will you step into the lift, Miss Terry?' said the receptionist, and pressed the button.

''Ullo, lass, back again?' said the commissionaire. 'Ben, are you drivin' t'young lady 'ome?'

''Op in, duck,' said Ben. ''Ow was Sam today? Was 'e nice to you?'

'Yes, he was,' said Ril.

'I should think so,' said Ben. 'I'd 'ave Sammed 'im if 'e 'adn't 'ave been.' And he let in the clutch.

*

'That was a splendid idea, Norman,' said Ril, 'to photograph those letters before they went back to Withishall. I'd never have thought of it myself in a month of Sundays.'

'And if he hadn't done that the whole matter would have been quietly buried,' said Hilda.

'And to think of sending them to Sam Thwaite!' Ril added. 'Hilda, the lad's a genius!'

'All right, all right,' said Norman, reddening. 'That's enough back-slappin' for now.'

Ril, back at Park Terrace, had been describing her interview with Sam Thwaite.

'What will you do now it's all over?' asked Hilda when she had finished.

'Well, my father seemed to think I was obsessed by all this,' said Ril thoughtfully. 'Maybe I have been. But there's lots of things I want to do before winter. I want to go some long walks on the moors. And I wish there was somewhere nice to swim.'

'I like walking,' said Hilda quickly. 'Let's go on some picnics.'

'Let's swim in some of them tarns,' suggested Norman.

'Let's all go to Leeds sometimes for a show,' said Hilda with a wild flight of fancy.

'Let's go dancin',' said Norman.

He met a look from Ril and added hastily, 'But not at t'Rex.'

'Yes, let's,' said Ril. For the first time since she had come North life seemed full and promising.

While they were talking Robert had been at the telephone. Now he came into the sitting-room beaming.

'I've fixed up a real change for you, Ril,' he announced. 'You can go and stay for a week with the Standishes in Belhampton. That is, if you want to.'

'Belhampton!' echoed Ril. 'Belhampton! If I want to!'

For weeks she had been too busy to feel any homesickness. But now it came over her in a great wave. The plans she had been making with Norman and Hilda seemed suddenly unimportant. There was only one thing she wanted in the world – the peace and loveliness of Belhampton.

'What a wonderful idea!' she cried. She ran to her father and kissed him. 'I just can't wait to start!'

Both Norman and Hilda looked crestfallen. But Ril could not have hidden her eagerness. She bubbled with joy.

'Belhampton!' she said again. 'Belhampton!' It was a poem in one word.

'I told them they could expect you on the train that gets in at three-thirty tomorrow, unless they heard otherwise,' said Robert. 'Martin will meet you. You'll have to leave Hallersage Station at nine-five tomorrow morning, so don't oversleep.'

'I can get up for that!' said Ril. 'I could get up at five for that!'

Already Caradoc and Withishall, and even Hallersage itself, were fading from her mind's eye, to be replaced by a vision of green Downs and chalky cliffs and the sleepy little town with its harbour and its boats and its beaches and the sea.

'I suppose this Martin's a pal of yours?' asked Norman.

'Martin Standish? Oh yes, he's ever such an old friend. I've known him since I was so high. We used to pinch apples together from Miss Denby's orchard. And he taught me to sail a boat.'

Norman looked gloomy.

'He's going up to Cambridge next term,' Ril added.

Norman's gloom deepened into a scowl.

'I suppose you have lots of friends in Belhampton,' said Hilda.

'Lots and lots,' said Ril. 'I just can't wait to see them again!'

At any other time she would have been more tactful. Norman and Hilda looked at each other wistfully. Ril was too excited to notice.

Then the doorbell rang.

Humming a tune, Ril ran down the steps. She opened the door smiling, ready to share her happiness with anyone

On the step stood Celia Withens. She looked white-faced and grim.

Ril recoiled.

'I'd like to speak to your father,' said Celia in flat tones.

'Y-yes, of course, Miss Withens. Will you come in?'

'By the way, I think this is yours.' Celia handed over a torch. 'It was found in the library.' She added with cold irony, 'If you ever take to a life of crime you'll have to be more careful.'

Ril felt foolish, and blushed. She showed Celia up to the flat, where Robert greeted her formally.

'I'm very sorry about last night's escapade, Miss Withens,' he said.

'You didn't know about it?'

'Of course not. I wouldn't have allowed it.'

Celia looked at him thoughtfully.

'No,' she said, 'no, I suppose you wouldn't. Nevertheless, it happened.'

'As I say, I'm sorry. I've told Ril what I think. She won't do such a thing again.'

'I'm afraid,' said Celia, 'that once is more than enough. Could we have a word on our own, Mr Terry?'

'I think I'd prefer my daughter and her cousin to stay.'

'Oh, all right,' said Celia. 'It makes no difference. But don't expect me to mince my words on account of them.'

'I'd better go,' said Hilda hastily, and vanished. Ril and Norman exchanged apprehensive looks.

Celia walked to the window and lit a cigarette. Her manner was calm, but beneath it were signs of nervous strain.

'I've just seen Cassell,' she went on. 'Only this morning he told me the document found at Withishall was worthless. He advised me to ignore it. But now he says that great oaf Sam Thwaite is threatening all kinds of nastiness, and he thinks I should negotiate. It seems, Mr Terry, that your daughter and her friend slipped a copy of Thwaite, and of course he's making the most of it.'

For all Celia's careful control, her voice was rising slightly.

'I'm afraid I have no influence over Mr Thwaite,' said Robert mildly.

'Anyway,' Celia went on, 'both Thwaite and Cassell have miscalculated. Cassell tells me to negotiate because he cares for the family reputation. His father and grandfather were the Withens family lawyers before him. But you know, Mr Terry, I don't care for the family reputation as much as Cassell does. In fact . . .'

She paused. Ril had the impression that she was making her mind up as she went along.

'. . . . In fact I'm not going to sign anything. I'm going to tell them all to go to hell.'

''Ere!' put in Norman, tilting his chair forward. 'Aren't you *ever* going to see reason? Don't you realize they're not askin' you for owt that really matters? T'old Common's a thousand times more use to 'Allersage than it is to you!'

'Norman! I'd rather you didn't speak to Miss Withens like that!' said Robert.

Celia's anger was rising.

'I don't give a damn for the Common!' she cried, 'but I won't be made a fool of, don't you see? All my life people have tried to make a fool of me. Well, this time they're not going to.'

She stubbed out her cigarette.

'Why should I care about publicity?' she went on. 'I shan't be here. I've booked a seat on the night plane to Nice from Northern Airport tonight. The whole lot of you can do just what you think fit!'

There was a pause. Then Norman inquired brutally:

'What about Roy?'

Celia flung the cigarette-stub into the empty fireplace. For the moment there was little left of her dignity.

'What about Roy?' she echoed with bitter irony. 'This morning Mr Wentworth honoured me with a proposal of marriage.'

Ril sat up sharply.

'You turned 'im down?' said Norman.

'I turned him down.'

'Well, I'm glad you 'ad that much sense.'

'So then he made an alternative proposition. He offered me a major shareholding in Quality Cars (Hallersage) Ltd.'

'That was kind, wasn't it?' said Ril, 'when you'd just refused to marry him.'

'Gerr! Kind!' said Norman scornfully. 'You mean 'e wanted you to put money into 'is business?'

'Yes. He said it was a fine business but short of capital.'

'It's short of capital all right,' said Norman. 'I take it the answer was still "Nothin' doin'".'

'It was,' said Celia. The temper had gone from her voice, and she was recovering her poise, but the bitterness remained. 'You see, he was only wanting something, like all the rest. And I thought he liked me.' She was silent for a moment. 'I wonder if I'll ever learn.'

Ril rose from her chair.

'Oh, poor Miss Withens!' she said on impulse. 'I'm so sorry . . .'

Celia cut off her sympathy with a chilly look.

'Do you wonder, Mr Terry, that I heartily wish I'd never set eyes on your daughter? She brought all this on me.'

'But I never meant any harm . . .' Ril protested.

'I'm not interested in your intentions,' said Celia.

She turned to Robert again.

'I must go, Mr Terry, if I'm to pack my things and catch that plane. By the way, I'm afraid you'll be getting notice to quit before long. I find I need the flat for somebody else. My agent will write to you.'

'But, Miss Withens –'

'And I think you might be wise to consider a new school for your daughter. Perhaps it hadn't occurred to you that she and her cousin may not be able to stay at Hallersage Grammar School. After all, I shall have to report to the school on last night's incident.'

'Is that a threat, Miss Withens?'

'No more than Mr Thwaite's remarks are threats.'

Celia strode to the door. Ril made a move to see her out of the flat, but was waved aside.

'You know,' said Robert as she disappeared, 'although she's so dreadful, I still can't help feeling sorry for that poor girl.'

'If I was you, Cousin Bob,' said Norman, 'I'd save my sorrow for nearer home.'

He was looking at Ril, whose eyes had filled with tears. Everything was wrong after all. For the second time in half an hour she went to her father and threw her arms round his neck. This time it was not to thank him for an unexpected treat: it was to sob on his shoulder.

'There, there, love,' said Norman, ''Ave a good cry if it 'elps. But don't give up 'ope. I'm just goin' to t'telephone. I reckon Sam 'ad better know about this.'

'Sam Thwaite?' said Ril. 'What can he do?'

''E'll do summat!' declared Norman with confidence. 'If there's one person in 'Allersage that's a match for Celia Withens it's Sam Thwaite!'

14

After a minute or two Ril felt better and went to stand beside Norman as he telephoned.

'None o' that nonsense,' he was saying into the mouthpiece. 'Put me through to Sam Thwaite, an' no messin'.... 'Ullo. Sam? Norman Clough. Look, Sam, I'm ringin' you from Park Terrace. Miss Withens 'as just bin 'ere and she's catchin' t'night plane to Nice. And she says she won't sign owt. . . . Aye, Sam, that's all very well, but Cassell's not goin' to clap eyes on 'er . . . Aye, Sam . . . Aye, well, 'appen that'll do t'trick, if we're quick enough . . . We'll wait for you at t'corner o' t'Old Road. See you in a few minutes. So long, Sam.'

He put down the receiver.

'Sam says Cassell can 'andle 'er. When it comes to a pinch, 'e says, she'll do as she's told. And Cassell knows that 'Allersage will 'ave to 'ave t'Common sooner or later, and 'e'd rather she 'anded it over now an' saved a lot of fuss. Sam says 'e'll pick up Cassell now, an' drive 'im to Withishall, collectin' us on t'way. 'E says if Celia doesn't toe t'line within t'next hour 'e's a Dutchman.'

'What about the threat to report us to the school? And to throw Daddy and me into the street?'

'She won't do it.'

'I'm not so sure.'

'Well, I'm tellin' you. Now, Ril, put your coat on. Sam's pickin' us up at t'corner of Old 'Allersage Road. 'E says we might be needed to illustrate 'is arguments, like.'

'I never thought I'd go to Withishall again,' said Ril.

It was nine o'clock and getting dark, and the nights were beginning to be chilly. Ril was glad of her warm coat. She and Norman stamped their feet and peered impatiently at every car that approached up the Old Hallersage Road. An age seemed to pass without any sign of Sam Thwaite. And when at last the Rolls-Royce drew up silently beside them it somehow managed to catch them unawares.

There were three people in the back: Sam himself; an elderly man who was obviously Mr Cassell; and a younger one whom Norman and Ril knew well.

'It's James!' said Ril to Norman. 'Whatever's he doing here?'

'Well, 'e's a Corporation lawyer,' said Norman. 'I expect this kind of 'ow-do-you-do is 'is business.'

They squeezed into the front beside the driver.

''Ullo, lass,' said Ben. 'There's no gettin' away from you today, is there? I don't know what's come over Sam. "Withis'all, as fast as you can," 'e says. "All right, Sam," I says, "we're not in t'pictures, you know. I'm not goin' to jigger that gearbox for you nor nobody else, Sam Thwaite," I says. "To 'ell wi' t'gearbox," 'e says, "you'll do as you're told." "Now look 'ere, Sam Thwaite," says I –'

A roar came from the back.

'Put thi foot down, Ben! We're in a 'urry!'

'All right, Sam, all right,' said Ben testily. He accelerated to a steady thirty. The Rolls was now leaving Old Haller-sage market-place and heading up the road to Withishall.

'For cryin' out loud!' muttered Norman in Ril's ear. 'Two speeds, slow an' stop!'

As they approached the Withishall gates, a car swung out into the road and passed them with headlamps full on and undipped.

'It's 'er!' cried Norman. 'It's Miss Withens in t'Jag!'

'Turn round, Ben,' ordered Sam. 'Foller that car. Don't let it get away!'

'Eh?' said Ben, bewildered. 'Eh, I don't know what next!'

'Get to the back, Ben!' came a commanding voice from behind. It was James. 'I'll drive!'

In a few seconds Ben was bundled into the back of the Rolls, and James took the wheel. Rapidly he turned in the road and shot smartly downhill after the disappearing tail of the Jaguar.

Celia's car was going fairly fast, but nothing like so fast as it could have done. Clearly she had not realized she was being followed. James was only just behind her as she crossed the market-place. Re-entering the Old Hallersage Road he missed the traffic-lights and Celia got a start, but James kept her in sight. Half a mile down the road she turned right into Pennine Road, heading for Lancashire and for Northern Airport.

'She's two hours to catch the plane,' said James. 'Plenty of time if you're in a Jag. I only hope she doesn't put her foot down. With a bit of luck we'll overtake her on the next long straight.'

The road was now winding up and round the hillside, with all the lights of Hallersage spread out below, but only the darkness and the tail-lamps of the Jaguar above. Ril glanced at the dashboard and saw that the Rolls was doing nearly fifty. On a winding uphill road it was a good speed. James's eyes were now fixed firmly on the road ahead, and he gripped the wheel grimly. Apart from some ruthless cornering there was no sign of haste. Regularly the tail-lights of the Jaguar disappeared as it rounded a bend, and regularly they reappeared as the Rolls followed.

'We've just about enough in reserve,' said James. 'Here goes.'

As they entered a long straight stretch James put his foot down and pulled out. The red lights of the Jaguar came nearer, as if it were being drawn backwards on a string.

'Let's 'ope she doesn't decide she's not goin' to be over-taken,' said Norman. 'That'd be just like 'er !'

But Celia allowed the Rolls to go past without changing her speed. Not far in front was a lay-by. James cut in ahead of the Jaguar, slowed down and hooted furiously.

'God 'elp us, she'll ram us up t'rear !' called Sam.

He was wrong. James had calculated well. Celia turned left into the lay-by. James pulled up with a screech of tyres, reversed, and shot into the lay-by in front of her.

Celia had jumped out of her car.

'What on earth is all this about?' she began.

From the back of the Rolls stepped, heavily, Mr Thomas Cassell, Solicitor, and Alderman Samuel Thwaite, Justice of the Peace.

Astonishment and then anger showed on Celia's face.

'We're sorry to bother you like this, Miss Withens,' said Sam in a conciliatory tone. 'But you left rather sudden, like, and me and Mr Cassell wondered if we could just 'ave a word with you.'

For the moment Celia seemed to be struggling to keep calm. She looked grim but said nothing.

'Now listen, my dear,' said Mr Cassell. He spoke as if to a naughty little girl. 'Don't get into one of your tantrums. You know I've always done my best for you, ever since you were so high. . . .'

Celia lit a cigarette and drew hard on it.

'Today I told you what I thought we should do about the old Common,' Mr Cassell went on. 'I said it would be best in the circumstances to let the town buy it at a fair market price. I want you to take that advice, Celia, because it's in your own interest. I've drawn up a letter authorizing Cassell and Sons to act on your behalf, and if you'll just sign here . . .'

It was touch and go. For a moment it seemed that the habit of years would be too strong for Celia and that Mr Cassell's governessy manner would carry the day. He was holding out his pen in every expectation that she would sign.

Then her face changed. She drew again on her cigarette and threw it down, threequarters unsmoked. A fresh, furious impulse took hold of her.

'I've listened to you too damned long!' she snapped. 'I'm not signing anything! I'm sick of you, and Hallersage, and England! I'm going, and I'm not coming back!'

'Celia! Just a minute . . .' began Mr Cassell patiently.

It was no good.

Celia slid behind the wheel of her car and let in the clutch. The Jaguar shot forward. Sam Thwaite, James, and Norman jumped for their lives. Celia swerved wildly into the main road, accelerated, and roared away towards the west and the airport.

Mr Cassell shook his head.

'My firm's acted for the Withens Estate for over a century,' he said. 'To think it had to fall into hands like hers!'

From somewhere above came a screech of brakes and then the roar of the throttle as the Jaguar snaked along the next stretch of road, up and round towards the mountains.

'Get back in, gentlemen,' said James quietly. 'I'm going to follow.'

'Don't be so daft, Jim!' said Sam Thwaite. 'We can't catch 'er at that speed. And we've no right to stop 'er if we did.'

'I wasn't thinking of catching her,' said James. He looked up at the dark winding road above. 'I was thinking that we might be needed.'

*

The Rolls-Royce drove on through the night at a steady forty. Ril felt apprehension mounting within her. Celia and the Jaguar had long been out of sight. James sat stern and upright at the wheel. In the back Sam Thwaite and Mr Cassell muttered inaudibly. Ben had shrunk into a corner. Norman on her left was grimly silent. Ril groped for his hand and held it.

They were heading for the Top Pass into Lancashire. On their right all the time was the mountainside, growing ever higher and steeper. On the left, most of the way, were sheer drops.

It was difficult driving. The road was never straight for half a mile at a time. Several dangerous bends were marked by white-painted fencing and rows of red reflectors.

James slowed for a specially treacherous corner. And there the headlights showed a jagged gap in the palings. On either side of the gap, surviving bits of fence hung down at drunken angles.

'That looks new,' said James ominously.

The Rolls drew to a stop. James and Norman got out. Ril followed them to the gap.

The night was black now. No stars could be seen, no light from farm or cottage. James had left the headlamps on, but the beam shone uselessly out into space. In front of their feet the ground fell away sharply. Ril felt she was on the brink of nothing.

For a minute or two everyone stood silent. Then, far below, was a phut – a muffled undramatic sound like a damp firework. Ril peered in its direction but could see nothing; the darkness was so complete that she might as well have been blindfolded.

Then came a distant spurt of flame – so small at first it seemed no more than if someone had struck a match. Quickly it grew to a blaze, but it was still so remote and silent that Ril's mind could hardly grasp what her eyes were telling her, until a sudden flare-up threw into relief the outline of the Jaguar, perched at a crazy angle in a watercourse far down the hillside.

'Come on, Norman,' said James quietly. 'We'd better see what we can do.'

Norman was through the gap already, slithering on the gravelly slope.

'I'm coming too,' said Ril.

'Me an' all,' said Sam Thwaite.

'There's no need for anyone else to come,' said James. 'Tell Ben to drive back to the last A.A. box and ring the ambulance, then the police. Then come back here so they'll know the place.'

'Aye,' said Sam reluctantly. 'Aye, 'appen you're right, Jim. Good luck. Now, where's t'lass?'

'You don't need me, Mr Thwaite,' said Ril. And she

162

followed James and Norman through the gap in the fence.

'Go back!' hissed James.

'I won't!'

'We shan't wait for you. What if you sprain your ankle or something?'

'I'm not going to.'

James said no more. He and Norman, scrambling and slipping, soon left Ril far behind. She began to think she had been rash. It was perilous going. Below the banking of the road the gravel gave way to heather, wet and slippery. She tried to stay upright, running down the hillside with little tottery steps, but soon her feet slid from under her and she skidded several yards on her bottom.

Grabbing wildly at handfuls of heather, Ril halted herself. The curve of the hillside now hid the flames of the burning car, but she heard James's voice calling to Norman. She picked herself up and headed uncertainly in their direction. Soon the ground began to feel boggy, and water came over her shoes. She was stumbling through a rivulet. And then the blazing car came into view again, but much nearer, and instead of the treacherous heather there was short sparse grass underfoot. Ril ran – slowly at first, then faster and faster until she was going almost too fast to stop. A few yards from the fire James fielded her with outstretched arms.

The Jaguar was well ablaze now.

'Is she in there?' cried Ril, horrified.

'No. Must have been thrown out.'

'Where is she, then?'

'Don't know. Somewhere on the hillside.'

Ril looked upward. Though her eyes were now accustomed to the dark, she could see little but the looming mass of the hill and the lights of two or three cars on the road far above.

'There's nowt we can do down here,' said Norman.

'We'll work our way uphill again,' said James. 'Ril, you

go off to the left. Norman, keep on my right. We'll cover as much ground between us as we can. If you see anything, Ril, don't go too near – just call to me.'

They set off. Ril was wet and tired now, and her hands were hurting because the scars caused by the bell-rope had reopened when she grabbed the heather on the way down. Soon she began to feel cold as well. Her sodden clothes clung to her and her feet squelched in her shoes at every step. Doggedly but in a daze she trudged up the steep slope. Every few minutes, James called, first to her and then to Norman.

They were nearly back to the road when Ril thought she saw a glimmer of something light-coloured over to her left. It was so dark that she could not be sure, but she made towards it.

Yes, she was right. Bedded in the thick heather was an unmistakably human figure.

'James!' she called. 'James! James!'

James came running across. Ril could hardly bring herself to look. But when she did there was nothing horrible about the sight. Celia lay face down, as if resting, with an arm curved above her head. James dropped to his knees beside her and felt for the pulse in her wrist.

'She's alive, Ril!' he said quietly.

Above on the road were now the clustered lights of three or four vehicles, and Ril could hear voices.

'T'ambulance'll be there by now, 'appen,' said Norman. He let out a piercing whistle. Somebody responded from above. Torches flickered. There was a clatter of equipment. Orders were called out.

James, still kneeling beside Celia, struck a match and held it between cupped hands. And seeing the beautiful unconscious face Ril wept. She wept with joy and dread, for Celia and for herself. She wept for the living flesh, warm among wet heather on the cold mountainside.

164

'Help me put my coat over her,' said James. 'Gently now. Gently. And now go back to the car. You've done your share for tonight.'

Norman was shouting instructions to the little knot of men now making their way down from the road. Ril passed them unnoticed going in the other direction. Somebody helped her up through the gap in the fence, and she stood uncertainly in the light of torches and headlamps.

And then up the road came a familiar sound. Ril would have known that engine anywhere. Daisy chugged past the line of parked vehicles and pulled in to the verge: and Robert Terry caught his daughter in his arms.

*

Ril sat propped up in bed and drank warm milk with rum in it. A hot-water bottle warmed her toes.

Her father came in from telephoning.

'Miss Withens is detained in Hallersage Royal,' he said. 'She has concussion and a few bruises. That's all, so far as they can tell at the moment. Sounds like a miracle to me. Anyway, she should be all right.'

'Thank goodness for that,' said Ril. 'Oh, thank goodness for that !'

'I wonder if it's too late at night to ring Henry Standish,' said Robert, 'and tell him you won't be going to Belhampton tomorrow.'

'Won't I?'

'Of course not. You need a good rest.'

'I'd rather go,' said Ril. 'There's nothing wrong with me. I could dance a jig right now.'

'I wouldn't try it if I were you,' said Robert. He looked at her thoughtfully. 'Still,' he said, 'if you do feel fit in the morning perhaps you might as well go. It'll do you good. And if you stay here in Hallersage you'll only be worrying.'

'About our notice to quit and all that?' said Ril. 'Yes, I suppose I will. I wonder what will happen?'

'We probably won't hear anything for a few days. So just you go away and put it right out of your mind. Have a lovely time in Belhampton. Good night, Ril.'

'Good night, Daddy. Bless you.'

This time Ril had none of James's pills to help her. But it made no difference. She slept like a stone.

15

As the train ran south, Hallersage dwindled in Ril's mind, and her worries dwindled with it. Robert had given her money to have lunch in the restaurant car. After lunch the countryside seemed to grow greener and softer every minute. The sun shone. Belhampton was getting nearer. Her heart sang along the lines.

Belhampton was at the end of a branch-line. There was a shuttle service by diesel car from the main-line junction. Belhampton station was no more than a single platform and a gaily painted wooden hut. It was high above the town, and as soon as Ril stepped outside she could see right across the bay.

Both town and bay lay washed in a pale September sunshine. The sea was blue but hazy, and she could just see across to the headland. The view was delicate, feminine, Southern.

Martin Standish was not at the station. Having only a light holdall, Ril waved the local taxi aside and started to walk. At a quarter to four in the afternoon time was no object. It was a still, mild day; late summer with a hint of autumn. Leaves were beginning to turn yellow.

She went round the corner into Bay Road, near her own old house. There was a seat where she had often sat looking down over the town. She picked out the old familiar landmarks. The church of honey-coloured stone: so different from the rugged grey slabs that reared up to form Old Hallersage Church. The elegant Georgian vicarage with its long green lawns. The market square and the famous Colonnade. Nightingales, her former school, with its Wren tower and the creeper ablaze on its walls. Everything seemed more beautiful even than she had remembered.

Ril set off downhill into the town. In the High Street she met Philippa Carey, who had been in her form at school.

''Lo, Ril,' said Philippa. 'Thought you'd gone away.'

'So I have,' said Ril. 'I'm only visiting.'

'Staying long?'

'A week.'

'Oh, good, I might be seeing you. Can't stop now. 'Bye, Ril.'

On the Colonnade Ril stopped to buy hair-grips at Waring's. She was friendly with the assistant there. But the girl she knew had left or gone on holiday. The new girl looked at her with blank lack of interest. She changed her mind and went out.

The tables were still outside Granby's café on the Square. Here Ril had spent many a summer hour talking to friends and watching the world go by. Now she ordered herself a lemonade and sipped it at leisure, observing the passing scene with an enjoyment which was not quite as great as she had expected. The world was still going by, but it seemed to consist entirely of strangers. The people she saw and heard were not as interesting as she would once have found them. And there was something odd about their accents – they sounded flat and lifeless after the rough vigour of expression she had got used to in Hallersage.

Little by little the joy of homecoming was ebbing away.

From where she sat she could see a gentle curve of down-land flowing down to the chalky cliff. This was a sight she had always loved. But even as she watched it was replaced in her imagination by the bleak windswept moorland of the West Riding. Here in Belhampton on this quiet day of early September everything stood still, even time. But there: how things moved, how you were alive!

Ril picked up her bag and set off, climbing now, on the walk to the Standishes' house at Belhampton West. Half-way up she was overtaken by a new Rover with Mr Standish himself at the wheel.

'Hop in, Ril!' he said. 'Good heavens, walking! And by yourself! Didn't that villain Martin meet you after all?'

'He probably didn't know what train I'd be on,' said Ril.

'Of course he knew. I told him myself. I expect he's gone off somewhere with Joanna Wood.'

'Joanna Wood!' repeated Ril, aghast. 'That mincing little piece! . . . Oh, I'm sorry, Mr Standish, perhaps I oughtn't . . .'

'Don't worry, Ril,' said Henry Standish, smiling faintly. 'I'm inclined to agree with you. But Martin seems to like her.'

'Well!' said Ril. 'Well!' And she lapsed into silence. If she had been here, she asked herself, would this have happened? Honesty gave her the answer: probably it would.

From Henry's house Ril telephoned Gillian, her former best friend. They had exchanged several letters during Ril's first weeks in Hallersage, but since then the correspondence had shown signs of drying up.

'Why, Ril!' said Gillian. 'How lovely! I just can't wait to see you.'

'I'll be round first thing in the morning,' said Ril.

'Fine. Actually it's the start of the junior tennis tournament, and we're all in it – all the gang, you know. You can come and watch, can't you?'

'I don't watch tennis much,' Ril said.

'No, well, of course you don't have to. But it's going to keep us all pretty busy for a few days. Look, why don't you come round to our house tomorrow evening? No, I forgot, it's Janet's party.'

'Who's Janet?'

'Oh, of course, you wouldn't know her. She's new here. She came just after you left. You'd like her – she's ever so nice. I wonder if I could ask her to invite you? Perhaps not. Well, never mind, Ril, I've got your number. I'll ring you later when I find out how things are. 'Bye, Ril.'

''Bye, Gillian,' said Ril. She put down the receiver and looked at it ruefully.

Martin and Joanna came in for supper, rather late. They seemed much taken with each other. Martin had started smoking a pipe, in readiness for his career as an undergraduate. Ril, who had admired him uncritically for as long as she could remember – he was three years her senior – now found herself for the first time weighing him up, and deciding that he was really rather an ordinary young man.

A slight pang of jealousy at seeing him so friendly with Joanna soon left her. But the three of them did not get on very well together. Ril snapped at Martin for retailing old jokes about Hallersage. Then Martin claimed to detect Yorkshire tones in her voice – at which Ril snapped again, not because it wasn't true but because she didn't see anything to laugh about if it was.

After supper Martin and Joanna went out for a walk. Ril wandered into the garden. She thought of another evening, only a few months earlier, when she had first learned that she was to leave Belhampton. Then she had cried into her pillow. Now nothing was the same. She had loved Belhampton, and perhaps in a way she still loved it and always would.

But it belonged to the past. She couldn't have it back. She didn't want it back.

Since the moment she arrived she had felt there was something missing from this remembered landscape. Now she realized what it was. What was missing was herself. She didn't belong here any more. She wanted – she wanted badly – to be in Hallersage.

Ril turned to find Henry Standish beside her. He was a tall, distinguished-looking man. Friendly, but a shade pompous. Nice, but (in spite of all the years she had known him) a stranger.

'Penny for your thoughts,' he said.

'I was thinking,' said Ril, 'that I can't really stay all week after all. You wouldn't mind, would you, if I went home on Monday morning?'

16

Norman stood with Robert Terry outside the barrier at Hallersage Station. He was impatient because Ril's train was five minutes late. He hadn't seen her for three whole days. That was less than the original week she was to have been away, but it was too long. Each morning he had mooched about the house until an impatient Florrie sent him packing. In the evenings he had spent hours with books that Ril had lent him, but whether because they interested him or simply because they were hers he could not have said. He had told himself again and again that it was daft to get into this state about a mere girl.

Now at the station he worried in case there had been some subtle change – in case, perhaps, she had returned in spirit to the South. His heart beat faster when at last he caught sight of her and saw her wave. She looked so small and slim among the crowd on the platform; she looked as if she needed protecting. Norman ached to protect her.

He stood beside her father and received in his turn an embrace – affectionate if cousinly. (But she was only a fourth cousin, Norman reminded himself; that didn't count.)

''Ow was Belhampton?' he asked when they were sitting together in the back of Robert's decrepit car.

'Oh, just as it always was. It's a lovely place, Norman. You ought to see it.'

'Did it make you wish you was back?'

'No.'

'No?'

'No, not at all. Quite the reverse.'

''Ow come, if you like it so much?'

'I live here now,' said Ril simply.

'An' what about Martin?'

'Oh, he's very well. He smokes a pipe now – or tries to. He's a funny boy.'

'Do you like 'im better than me?' demanded Norman jealously.

Ril laughed.

'Oh, Norman, how silly! I haven't thought of it like that.'

She saw that he found the reply disappointing and went on :

'No, as a matter of fact I don't. I like you much better. Anyway, Martin's got a girl-friend. Her name's Joanna.'

'Good luck to Joanna!' said Norman with fervour.

*

Daisy turned from the Old Hallersage Road into Park Terrace. Drawn up before the gate of No. 5 was a vehicle that had become familiar.

'It's that Rolls again!' said Ril.

Sam Thwaite's chauffeur, Ben, leaned against the bonnet eating chips out of a newspaper.

'It's as well you've come,' he said. 'Sam's in your flat, an' 'e dun't like to be kept waitin'.'

'How did he get in?' asked Robert, staring.

'We found t'key under t'mat, o' course,' said Ben, 'where keys always is.'

'For a man of high I.Q.,' said Ril to her father, 'you haven't much imagination in hiding a door-key. It's a good job we're not worth burgling.'

They went upstairs. Sam was installed in the best arm-chair and had found himself a drink.

'Well, this is an honour, Mr Thwaite,' said Robert drily.

'It is an' all,' agreed Sam. 'It's not everyone in 'Allersage that gets a visit from Sam Thwaite, I can tell you.'

He studied Robert with interest.

'So you're t'lass's dad,' he went on. 'You've got a good lass there. Bit o' right Yorkshire in 'er. Wants watchin', though. I wouldn't stand no nonsense from 'er if I was you.'

Sam puffed at his pipe contentedly.

'Anyroad,' he said, 'I came to give you some news. Me an' Tom Cassell's been to see Miss Withens today in 'Allersage Royal. An' it's just like I said. Tom can 'andle 'er if 'e gets 'alf a chance. She was as meek as a cooin' dove to-day.'

Sam reconsidered his last remark and then amended it: 'Well, nearly as meek. An' now it's all settled, and t' trans-fer o' t'Common'll go through just like I said it would. When Sam Thwaite tells you owt you can count on it.'

'And what about our notice to quit?' asked Ril.

'Aha,' said Sam. 'That's all been fixed up, too. Guess who by.'

'Sam Thwaite.'

'That's right. You're a bright lass, aren't you? Want to know 'ow I did it?'

'Yes, please.'

'Well, I says to our little Celia, I says, "Miss Withens, do you know 'ow many units of accommodation I control in 'Allersage?" She says, "No." I says, "Six 'undred an' forty-two." She says, "Oh." I says, "An' do you know what's t'simplest thing in t'world for me?" She says, "What?" I says, "To find somebody a better 'ome than the one what they're bein' thrown out of." She says, "Do you mean . . .?" I says, "Yes, I do." I says, "If you throw t'Terrys out you won't be doin' them no 'arm, you'll just be losin' good tenants an' makin' a bad name for yourself." '

Sam paused and sucked at his pipe.

'So then she says: "Oh well, I never meant to do it anyway, it was only to give 'em a fright. I shall let t'matter drop." I says: "That's right, duck, you'd better. An' what's more," I says, "while ever I'm chairman o' t'governors, anyone who wants to throw them two kids out of 'Allersage Grammar School will 'ave to throw me out first." So then she says: "I don't want 'em thrown out, it's nothin' to me. In fact," she says, "I'm throwin' myself out, because I'm goin' to resign from t'governors." "You might as well," I says, "for all t'good you've ever done." "All right, Sam Thwaite," she says, "if you're goin' to start gettin' personal I can tell you a thing or two . . ." '

But at this point Sam saw fit to end his narrative.

'Anyway, how is Miss Withens?' Ril asked.

'Oh, she's fine,' said Sam. 'It's a bloomin' marvel, if you ask me! You wouldn't 'a' thought she'd a cat in 'ell's chance. An' there she is, as large as life, with nobbut a few bruises.'

'You don't know how thankful I am,' said Ril. 'If she'd been killed I'd never have forgiven myself.'

'Nay, lass,' said Sam, 'it wouldn't 'a' been your fault, whatever 'appened. That Celia was born to trouble. She's spent 'er life takin' corners too fast, in a manner o' speakin'.'

'Maybe this'll shake 'er out of it,' suggested Norman.

'Aye, well, I wish it would,' said Sam with a sigh. 'It'd be a good thing for 'Allersage if she'd settle down an' get wed to a good steady chap as'd keep 'er in order.'

'That doesn't sound like our Celia,' said Ril. 'And yet, you know, she must feel she has roots here. It wouldn't be so very astonishing if she came home for good some day....'

As she was speaking, Ril heard voices outside on the landing, and then footsteps going up to the flat above. And an inspiration struck her, cutting across the train of her thoughts.

'Come along, Mr Thwaite!' she cried eagerly. 'Come and see the Hallersage of tomorrow!'

'I've enough to do wi' t'Allersage of today,' grumbled Sam.

But he followed obediently up to James Willoughby's flat. James was there, and Kenneth Ryder, the architect, and Kenneth's fiancée, Barbara Carr.

''Ullo, Jim,' said Sam. ''Ullo, Ken, built any nice rabbit-'utches lately? 'Ullo, young woman. I don't know your name, but you're t'one at t'art school that teaches 'em to draw folk wi' six eyes an' three noses, aren't you? Never forget a face, that's Sam Thwaite.'

'This way, please, Mr Thwaite,' said Ril sweetly and led him into the other room.

And there in all its glory was Kenneth's model of the New Hallersage. There, as before, were the breathtaking new buildings – some tall and dramatic, some long and low and arcaded, all light and airy with acres of glass. There were the paved squares and the gardens and the bandstand, and the toy traffic routed round a wide circular road with bridges over it for pedestrians.

Sam Thwaite wandered round it with eyebrows raised. Then he looked at Kenneth with new respect.

'Well, I don't know much about architecture,' he said, 'but I didn't rise from a barefoot lad to t'chap I am today wi'out bein' able to recognize one thing. An' you know what that is? Imagination.'

He warmed to the theme.

'Aye, Sam Thwaite can tell a good idea a mile off. An' you know what this 'ere model is? It's daft, it's fantastic, an' every man but one in 'Allersage would say it's impossible. But Sam Thwaite says no, it's not impossible. It's brilliant an' it can be done.'

He took another hard look at the model.

'There's a 'ell of a lot o' glass in it, isn't there, young Ken?'

'Too much glass,' said Barbara promptly.

'Take no notice of her, Mr Thwaite,' said Kenneth. 'She knows no more about architecture than you do.'

Sam raised his eyebrows, offended. James intervened hastily.

'Of course, it would cost a lot of money,' he said.

''Ow much, Jim?'

'You could make a start with five or six millions.'

Ril waited for Sam to recoil in horror. But he scratched his head and pondered for a moment.

'Aye,' he said, 'but not much of a start. Lots o' compensation to pay before you could lay a single brick. (Does it use any bricks, Ken?) We'd need more than that. Never mind. When it comes to raisin' a few millions there's no one to beat Sam Thwaite.'

'I believe you,' said James.

'Mind you,' Sam added hastily, 'I'm not promisin' owt. I'm only sayin' I'll do my best.'

'And if there's one man whose best's worth doing it's Sam Thwaite,' concluded Ril.

'Why, you cheeky tuppence . . .' began Sam.

Norman had been studying the model silently while this was going on.

'I don't like it,' he announced. 'It isn't 'Allersage. Why,

it might be anywhere in t'world. 'Allersage is a place on its own. It should keep its own character.'

Ril was cross. She had thought this one out for herself.

'Now listen, Norman,' she said. 'First, it'll keep the best buildings of the present town. Second, it does belong to Hallersage, because a Hallersage man designed it and all being well Hallersage men will build it. And thirdly, my lad, the character of this town doesn't depend on bricks and mortar, or on stone and soot for that matter. It depends on the people who live here!'

'Well said, lass!' declared Sam.

But Ril was waiting for Norman's counterblast.

He frowned as he pondered her words. It was some time before he spoke. And when he did he startled her.

'Maybe you're right, Ril,' he admitted meekly.

17

The smell of Sunday dinner filled the kitchen. Florrie's red face glistened as she bustled about, juggling with saucepans, setting out knives and forks, and accompanying herself with a nonstop running commentary. The climax of the week was at hand.

A blast of hot air vibrated through the room as she opened the oven door.

'Done to a turn!' she announced, beaming. 'As nice a bit o' brisket as ever I saw. Now, where's that lad got to? Fred, go and give our Norman a shout. Ril love, sit you down over there. Get yourself outside some Yorkshire puddin'. Build you up a bit, that will. None o' your foreign nonsense 'ere.

'Oh, 'ere comes t'lad. Let's look at your 'ands. Aye, an'

yours too, Fred Clough. I thought so. Mucky as sin. Go an'
get 'em washed, both of you. An' be quick an' all. Don't
you wait for 'em, Ril love. Get on an' eat it before it spoils.
We can't keep t'guest of honour waitin'.'

'Allow me, Miss Terry,' said Norman. ''Ave some
Château Whatnot, 1949. Guaranteed pure H_2O.' He poured
her some water.

'Well now,' said Florrie happily. ''Earty congratulations,
Ril love. I can tell you we're all proud of you, in spite o'
them doubts what Fred 'ad. I knew when I first clapped eyes
on you – I said to myself, that's a right clever lass, I said.
To think you found old Caradoc's letter in no time, when
none of us 'ad done owt about it all them years. An' now
Norman says t'old Common's comin' back to 'Allersage.
'Ere, Fred, why don't you say summat?'

''Aven't you said enough for both of us?' demanded Fred.

'Well, I like that!' said Florrie. 'I'd 'a' thought you might
'ave 'ad a word o' thanks for t'lass.'

'Thanks?' said Fred. 'What 'ave I got to thank 'er for?
This 'orrible great park comin' to t'town, and costin' a fortune no doubt, an' it'll all go on to t'rates, as if t'rates wasn't
'igh enough already. I've said it before an' I'll say it again :
it's time t'lass learned to leave things alone that don't concern 'er.'

'Aw, give it a rest, Dad,' said Norman. 'It's folks like you
that keeps t'place 'alf dead. If you want things to 'appen
you've got to go out an' make 'em 'appen. An' I reckon Ril
does that all right.'

Fred wasn't listening. A further thought had occurred to
him.

'An' what's more,' he said, 'do you know this town loses
eight thousand a year already on t'trams? An' think of all
t'thousands o' tram journeys made every year by children
goin' up to t'sports fields on Leeds Road. All that income'll
be lost. T'trams'll be further than ever in t'red.'

'Trams is bein' abolished,' said Norman. 'Didn't you see it in t'*Chronicle* yesterday?'

'Oh, what a shame!' cried Ril. 'The nicest things on the road!'

''Igh time they went,' said Norman. 'Been obsolete for years.'

'There's nowt wrong wi' t'trams!' declared Fred.

'Slow an' cumbersome!' shouted Norman. 'Get in t'way o' t'traffic!'

'Safe as 'ouses!' shouted Fred. 'Cheapest form o' transport!'

'I love them!' shouted Ril over the top of them both.

'Now then,' said Florrie placidly. 'Get on wi' your dinners, all of you, an' stop arguin'.'

There was a tap on the door. The nurse from Great-Aunt Martha's house put her head round.

'I've brought someone to see you,' she said.

Into the room, walking uncertainly but unaided, came the little frail figure of Aunt Martha herself.

'There! Isn't she well?' said the nurse proudly. 'First time she's been out since June! She can stay for half an hour, then I'll come back for her.'

Florrie rushed to put Aunt Martha into the rocking-chair, where she sat swaying gently. She had come for a purpose. She was quite alert.

'Where's t'lass?' she asked. 'Oh, there she is. Come to me, Margaret.'

'Not Margaret – Ril,' said Florrie patiently.

'I never 'eard of no such name,' said the old lady. 'I shall call thee Margaret, love, because thou'rt t'spitten image o' Margaret. It takes me back eighty year to look at thee.'

Ril went across and kissed her.

'You know what she's done, don't you, Auntie?' said Florrie.

'Aye,' said Aunt Martha. 'Aye, I know. I came to tell

thee, lass, 'ow my grandfeyther would 'a' loved thee. An' it's Caradoc Clough I'm talkin' about now. Thou'd 'a' been a lass after 'is own 'eart. "Brains an' spirit," 'e used to say, "that's what I like to see in a lass." 'E were allus fond o' Margaret.'

'I wish I could have known him,' said Ril.

'I wish 'e could 'a' seen this day,' said Aunt Martha wistfully. Then she brightened.

'But I'm glad I've seen it,' she went on. 'Eh, it's done me good, it 'as that! I felt that wore out, I couldn't be bothered wi' nowt no more. An' now I feel twenty years younger. An' listen, our Florrie, I'm goin' to live to be a 'undred. None o' t'Cloughs 'ave done it yet, that I know of. I'm goin' to show t'lot o' you!'

'Up the Cloughs!' said Ril.

'Eh, t'Cloughs!' said Florrie, shaking her head. 'My dad warned me about marryin' into that lot!'

'What's wrong wi' t'Cloughs?' demanded Fred, Norman, and Aunt Martha together.

'All t'Cloughs is stubborn,' said Florrie, 'an' all t'Cloughs thinks they knows best, an' none o' them teks no notice o' nobody else. Do you know, before you come in, Aunt Martha, they was all shoutin' each other's 'eads off about whether 'Allersage ought to keep t'trams.'

'T'trams,' repeated Aunt Martha thoughtfully. 'Aye well, t'old 'orse trams was all right. You could see what was pullin' 'em. But I never did think much to these 'ere electric things. They don't look natural to me. An' don't none o' you tell me nowt else, because I won't listen to you. . . .'

     *

'Why, it's Amaryllis! Come in, duck!' cried Mrs Woodward delightedly. She waddled ahead of Ril into the living-room at Milton Street. Music swirled from the teleradiogram. The room smelled of scent. Janet, in front of the looking-glass, was spraying her hair. Sylvie, in her under-clothes, was doing something to a dress. She held it up against herself as Ril went in.

'Will Roy like this?' she asked.

'Roy?'

'Yes, Roy. R-O-Y, Roy.'

'You're going to see him?'

'I thought you was the Great Brain. Yes, of course I'm goin' to see 'im, or I wouldn't be askin' you, would I? I've seen 'im every night this week.'

'I think he'll like the dress. But . . .'

'But what about Celia, you mean?' Sylvie half laughed, half jeered. 'That's all over. Finished. The end. She turned 'im down, you know.'

'And you'll take him on the rebound like that?' Ril asked.

'Aye,' said Sylvie. For a moment she looked bitter. 'Aye, I suppose I'm daft. An' I'll get no thanks from 'im, you know. 'E doesn't care.'

''E's treated 'er shockin',' said Mrs Woodward conversationally. ''Ow about a cupper tea?'

'Amaryllis 'as come to see 'Ilda,' Janet pointed out.

'Oh aye,' said Mrs Woodward. ''Ilda-a-a! Our 'Ilda-a-a! She'll be down in a minute, duck!'

'I'm here now,' said Hilda, appearing in the doorway.

Everyone looked up. Sylvie whistled. Hilda didn't look at all the grubby child who had appeared in the same door-way when Ril was in the house a few weeks before. She was dressed to go out, and her hair was brushed and her stockings were straight and she had put something on her face.

'That's all for Cliff's benefit,' said Janet, and giggled.

'Yes, our 'Ilda's got a boy-friend,' said Sylvie.

Hilda blushed.

'Cliff?' asked Ril. 'Not the lad who was with us at the Rex? The one with two left feet?'

180

'It seemed more like twelve left feet when 'e tried to dance wi' me,' said Sylvie.

'Now then, our Sylvie, don't make fun of 'im,' said Mrs Woodward. ''E's a right nice lad, is Cliff. Nicer than some I can think of.'

'Oh, leave off, can't you?' protested Hilda. 'It's all about nothing. Just because I went once to the pictures with him you have to make all this fuss.'

'Well, I must say it's smartened you up a bit,' said Sylvie.

'It's not Cliff that's smartened 'er up,' said Janet. 'I reckon it's since she got pally with Amaryllis 'ere.'

'It's none o' that,' said Mrs Woodward comfortably. 'It's just time passin', like. First they're babbies, then they're children, then they start growin' up, an' soon you can't do owt with 'em. That's t'way o' t'world. Now let's have that cupper tea.'

    *

'Hullo, lad,' said Roy. 'Looking for a job?'

'No,' said Norman. 'Are you?'

'What d'you mean?'

'I gather Miss Withens wouldn't part wi' any cash.'

'You know too much, don't you?' said Roy. They were in his tiny glass-walled office in a corner of the showroom, and Roy was keeping an eye on a prospective customer who wandered round among the cars. At exactly the right moment he would offer his assistance.

'If you think I can't carry on without Miss Withens's money,' he added, 'you're on the wrong track. It's a bit hand-to-mouth at the moment, I admit. You need capital to keep a stock of cars. But this is a good business, Norman lad. Miss Withens has missed her chance.'

'An' I suppose she missed another chance by not marryin' you?'

'Oh, that,' said Roy. 'I reckon that was an escape for me.

She's neurotic, you know. Neurotics aren't much fun. I'll have to look for another girl-friend. In the meantime there's always Sylvie.'

He was still watching the customer.

'That chap means business,' he said. 'I can always tell when they're serious. I'll give him another minute.'

He turned to Norman.

'You're not friendly to me these days, lad. If it's because of what happened at Withishall forget it. That's all over. And listen, why don't you think again about coming in with me? I'll pay you good wages, and as soon as you're twenty-one you can be a partner. You on the technical side and me on the sales – we'd make a good team.'

'Nothin' doin'.'

'Perhaps you're letting them keep you at school after all?'

'Nobody's keepin' me anywhere. But I'm stayin' at school, that's a fact. I think I'll sit for an engineerin' scholarship at West Ridin' University in two years' time. I was talkin' to old Scotty Ross, my form-master, the other day, an' 'e said I'd got a first-rate chance. An' then I could do real engineerin' – creative stuff, not just the old grease-an'-spray.'

'Looking well ahead, eh?' said Roy with a trace of sarcasm.

'Aye, well, that'll give me another two years in t'Sixth Form. There's lots you can do in t'Sixth Form that you'll never be able to do again. Old Scotty doesn't believe in over-specializin'. 'E says you should develop other interests as well. I might take up summat quite different on t'side.'

'Someone's been influencing you !' said Roy mischievously. Norman reddened.

'I make up my own mind,' he said.

'I don't doubt it. But even you can be helped, eh? Well, off you go, lad – unless you want to watch me do a bit of business.'

Roy shot his cuffs, straightened his tie, and advanced smiling upon the customer.

'Good morning, sir,' he said in the showroom accent. 'You'll forgive me for saying that I've been watching you for a minute or two. It's a pleasure to see a customer who knows what he's about. I could tell at once that yours was an expert eye. It wouldn't be any use trying to sell *you* a dud. But I'm sure we can find something that will come up to your standards . . .'

Roy was in his element. The pleasure of selling never palled.

                    *

It was the general visiting time at Hallersage Royal Infirmary. Celia was in a private ward – a biggish, sunny corner room with brightly polished parquet floor. Ril slithered across it towards the high white bed. Nobody else was there, and nobody seemed to be expected, for Celia lay listlessly looking at the ceiling.

'Hullo,' said Ril.

The blue eyes turned towards her.

'I just came to say I'm sorry,' said Ril. 'Or, rather, not that I'm sorry for what I did, but I'm sorry you've had such a bad time.'

'All right,' said Celia. 'Don't start tripping over your conscience. It doesn't matter.'

'Well, I sort of feel responsible for all this. . . .'

'I told you, it doesn't matter. You're no worse than the rest. I've been made a fool of again, that's all. It isn't the first time. I don't suppose it will be the last.'

'I forgot to ask how you are,' said Ril.

'I'm perfectly well. They're letting me out on Friday. I suppose I ought to thank you. It wouldn't have done me any good to lie on that hillside all night.'

'What will you do when you leave hospital?'

'I shall go. I don't want to see Withishall for a long long time.'

'Where will you go? Back to the South of France?'

'I don't know. I'm bored with France. I'm bored with Italy. I'm bored with everywhere. People keep talking about the Bahamas – I might go there.'

'You'll be bored in the Bahamas,' said Ril. 'You'll be bored wherever you go as long as you're always running away.'

'Oh, for God's sake!' said Celia in disgust. She raised herself on an elbow. 'What is it about me that makes people want to moralize? Even babes and sucklings! Go away, Ril Terry. I'm bored with you, too.'

'Just as you wish,' said Ril. 'Good-bye, Celia.'

She was halfway across the slippery floor when Celia called her back.

'You didn't ask me about the thing,' she said.

'What thing?'

'The old Common. Cassell was here the other day. I gave him power to negotiate. The town will get what it wants.'

'Yes, I know,' said Ril. 'Thank you.'

'Don't thank me, thank him. And Thwaite. And the great principle of moral blackmail.'

'It would have had to go eventually, wouldn't it?'

'I suppose so,' said Celia wearily. 'It's a kick in the teeth for the family motto, though. Oh well, I held on while I could. Good-bye, Ril. Thank you for calling. Don't bother to come again.'

'Perhaps I could see you some time when you're at Withishall?' Ril suggested.

Celia stared.

'I don't want anything,' Ril added hastily. 'Honestly I don't. I just thought it would be nice if I could call on you.'

'Do you know,' said Celia thoughtfully, 'do you know, in

spite of everything, I believe you. Yes, I'll be seeing you, Ril. I shall like that.'

Ril was thinking hard as she left the hospital for the sunshine outside.

'"*Quod teneo tenebo*",' she repeated to herself. 'What I have I hold.' It was a dreadful motto. And Ril realized that in some dim, half-understood way it had ruled Celia Withens's life. So far, at least, Celia could give nothing – least of all herself.

*

'Ril, do you mind?' said Robert. 'I've asked Miss Sadler to supper tomorrow night. Could you make something nice?'

'Leave it to me,' said Ril.

'We're going to complete the preparations for the social-history course. Term starts next week. And you know what – in view of your efforts we'll have to revise the last lecture. So we'll need your help.'

'Is there a lot of interest in the course?' Ril asked.

'Enormous. If we get many more enrolments we'll have to split it into two. And not only this one, Ril. It looks as if all the courses will be popular. The university are delighted.'

'Good for you, you old genius!' said Ril, and kissed him. 'So you think you made the right move in coming here?'

'So far as I'm concerned, I know I did,' said Robert. 'The only thing is . . .' He fell silent.

'I know,' said Ril. 'Don't worry, Daddy. I like it here.'

18

'Show me it again, Norman,' said Ril.

Norman passed her the newspaper. She took it in her mittened hands. Huddled in the raw cold air of Hallersage Moor they pored over it. It was a Saturday afternoon in November. The school term was more than half over. The events of the summer seemed far away. But the story in the *Hallersage Chronicle* brought them back:

'WITHENS LAND FOR HALLERSAGE'
'Old Common to provide Park and
Playing-fields'

'More than a thousand acres of the Withishall Estate will be handed over to Hallersage under an agreement announced today between the Corporation and Messrs. Cassell and Sons, solicitors to the estate.

'The Corporation will lay out a five-hundred-acre park with riverside walks, providing what was described yesterday as "a vital lung for Hallersage".

'In addition, playing-fields and pavilions will be provided for all schools and youth organizations on the western side of the town. When these are ready school-children will be spared the long journey to the existing playing-fields in Leeds Road.

'The purchase price is not disclosed, but Alderman Samuel Thwaite, who has led the negotiations for the Corporation, today described it as "extremely reasonable".

'Said Alderman Thwaite: "It is a splendid example of the unfailing public spirit of the Withens family, who have done so much for our town."

'It is understood that Miss Celia Withens gave her approval in principle to the transfer before leaving in September for a cruise in the Southern Hemisphere.'

Norman and Ril looked at each other. Ril turned up her coat collar, for it was getting colder. Below them, Hallersage could dimly be seen through its smoke-haze. The roar of a football crowd was borne to them intermittently on the wind.

'That old 'ypocrite Sam!' said Norman. 'Unfailin' public spirit o' t'Withenses! What next?'

'I suppose that's how they wrap these things up,' said Ril. 'Sam knows what he's about. He hinted once that he might finish up as Lord Hallersage.'

'I wouldn't be surprised if 'e did,' said Norman, 'what with all this and t'scheme for t'new town centre that Sam's pushin'. Oh aye, there's no flies on Sam!'

'Well, if he does become Lord Hallersage it's more than any of the Withenses did,' said Ril. 'I suppose there's poetic justice in it. Sam comes from one of the old village families, like ours. He says he has an ancestor who marched with Caradoc.'

'Then maybe t'title should 'a' come to us,' said Norman. He laughed. 'What was that sayin' of old Caradoc that you told me about?'

'I know it by heart,' said Ril. And she declaimed once more: '"By force and by fraud you have robbed us of our birthright, but this I declare – that what the folk of Hallersage have lost the folk of Hallersage shall one day recover!"'

There was a brief silence. Then Norman spoke, with awe in his voice.

'Today!' he said. 'That's t'day Caradoc spoke about. Today!'

'Poor Celia!' said Ril on impulse.

A louder, prolonged roar drifted up from the football match.

'Sounds like a goal for 'Allersage,' said Norman. He blew on his fingers and stamped his feet. Then he looked searchingly at Ril, seemed about to say something more, but finally bit his lip and stayed silent.

'What is it, Norman?'

'Oh, I was just thinking. About us.'

'What about us?'

'I was thinkin' you an' me might go out together.'

'Well, we do, sometimes.'

'I mean more often. I mean, sort of as if we were serious, like.'

Ril sighed.

'I think we're all right as we are,' she said. 'I hope you don't mind, Norman, but I don't feel serious. I don't feel ready to be serious.'

Norman frowned.

Ril went on, 'Let's just be friends, for now.'

His frown deepened.

'I do like you, Norman,' she added hastily. 'I like you ever so much. But that's how it is.'

Painfully, Norman managed to grin.

'Oh well,' he said, 'I suppose that's better than a kick in t'teeth. Come on, let's go an' 'ave some tea at Maggie's. I'll treat you.'

'Thank you,' said Ril. 'I'd like that.'

The mist was rising now, and the horizons drawing in. The town was almost lost in the haze. The long final whistle of the football match rose frailly to their ears, and the last roar of the crowd. Lights were going on everywhere. Ril could make out the illuminated outline of a tram adventuring westwards up the Old Hallersage Road.

She thought with pleasure of tea and toast and the friendly bustle of Maggie's café. It was time now to be with people: time for the Saturday crowds in the market-place and the shop-window gazers jamming the High Street.

The first time she had seen Hallersage she had thought how ugly it was. Now she felt differently. The town was part of the landscape and the landscape was part of the North, and the North could be ugly on the surface but was beautiful in the bone. Hallersage was her town. She meant to go everywhere and do everything, but she would come back to it.

'I belong here, Norman,' she said in wonder. 'Do you realize? I'm a Yorkshire lass now. Ee by gum, who would 'a' thowt it?'

'Get away wi' you!' said Norman. 'You a Yorkshire lass? Not in a 'undred years. To me you're t'South, an' allus will be.'

'Oh well,' said Ril, 'maybe it takes both of them to make a world.'

In her mind a wider idea was forming. It didn't just take North and South to make a world: it took all that they symbolized. It took both tough and tender, both practical and romantic. It took masculine and feminine.

Some day she would have to work it all out. But not now. It was getting chilly, up there on the moor. On impulse she broke into a run.

'You can't catch me!' she cried, and raced ahead of Norman on the path that led down to the town. 'You can't catch me!'

Norman thudded in pursuit. He could run faster, she knew. But she was confident that on these hilly paths she could give him the slip. She was sure-footed and elusive. He wouldn't catch her till she was ready to be caught.

If you have enjoyed this book and would like to know
about others, why not join the Puffin Club?
You will get a badge, *Puffin Post* four times a year,
and the right to enter all the competitions.
You'll find the application form overleaf

Application for membership of The Puffin Club

(Write clearly in block letters)

To :

The Puffin Club Secretary,
Penguin Books Ltd,
Harmondsworth,
Middlesex

I would like to join the Puffin Club. I enclose my 5s. membership fee for one year and would be glad if you would send me my badge and copies of *Puffin Post* four times in the year.

Surname...

Christian name(s)...

Full Address..

....

....

Age .... Date of Birth...

Where I buy my Puffins..

Signature of applicant...

Date ....

Note : We regret that at present applications for membership can be accepted only from readers resident in the U.K. or the Republic of Ireland.